DREAM ME

Kathryn Berla

Amberjack Publishing
New York, New York

Amberjack Publishing
228 Park Avenue S #89611
New York, NY 10003-1502
http://amberjackpublishing.com

Publisher's Cataloging-in-Publication
Names: Berla, Kathryn.
Title: Dream Me / by Kathryn Berla.
Description: New York, NY: Amberjack Publishing, 2017.
Identifiers: ISBN 978-1-944995-20-1 (pbk.) | 978-1-944995-28-7 (ebook)| LCCN 2016961110
Summary: Babe's dreams of the perfect guy begin to seem so real that she falls for him. Will her dreams become reality?
Subjects: LCSH Dreams--Juvenile fiction. | Time travel—Juvenile fiction. | Sexual harassment--Juvenile fiction. | Country clubs--Florida--Juvenile fiction. | Tennis--Juvenile fiction. | Florida--Fiction. | Love stories. | BISAC YOUNG ADULT FICTION / Romance / General | BISAC YOUNG ADULT FICTION / Time Travel.
Classification: LCC PZ7.B45323 Dr 2017 | DDC [Fic]—dc23

Cover Design: Dane Low

Row, row, row your boat
Gently down the stream
Merrily, merrily, merrily, merrily . . .

Zat

He thought about the girl again. The dark red color of her hair reminded him of the flaming sun at the very second it dropped out of sight. Such an odd color, really. And the mass of hair on her head . . . So silly and useless. What would it feel like to have that growth sprouting from your head? Hot, undoubtedly. What would it feel like to touch it? To run your fingers through it? He knew there were differences in the quality of hair, from coarse and thick, like rubbing sand between the palms of your hands, to smooth and slippery, like the inside of the juicy cactus plant. But which would hers feel like? He couldn't tell from the looks of it. He could never tell. He would never know.

Zat's uncle's chest rose and fell, and he could hear a heaviness in his breath that signified sleep. His uncle slept most of the time these days. All the older ones did, the ones who were staying behind. Zat knew he should sleep more, rest to be strong enough for what lay ahead. But he couldn't quiet his mind. He had so many questions that wouldn't leave him alone.

He leaned back against the wall and brought his lids down over his eyes, trying to force a dream. Outside the wind whined and moaned like a wounded beast, but inside his head he could retreat to the images of that long ago, almost mythical Earth. The words, written by a man people were no longer interested in—they'd inspired Zat to make the difficult choice of separating from his family, chasing a future they believed impossible, foolish—even suicidal. Now he called on those words to calm his nerves and boost his sagging courage.

The clouds over the land now rose like mountains and the coast was only a long, green line . . .

He forced his mind to a place where clouds once filled the sky. As high as mountains above him. What would that be like?

The water was dark blue now, so dark that it was almost purple . . .

A sea of rolling waves so vast it changed colors depending on the sun and the moon and the presence or absence of clouds. Now the deeply salted, toxic sea had only two colors: slate gray and black. At sunrise and sunset an orange glaze spread across its surface. But it had been many years since Zat had seen the sea. Nobody went there anymore. Nobody had any use for it apart from the greasy, lurking monsters that inhabited its depths.

"Zat?" his uncle turned and Zat wasn't sure for a

moment if he'd woken or was just mumbling as he often did while he slept.

"Yes, Uncle?"

"You're still here?"

"Yes, Uncle."

"Isn't there a gathering? It's not night yet, is it?"

"No, Uncle. It's not night. I didn't go."

"Why not go? You should be with other young people while you still can."

"There's no point. Everyone's leaving, and anyway, none of them want to have anything to do with me. They all think I'm crazy."

"And maybe you are . . . maybe you are. There's still time to change your mind."

"And what? Leave here hoping to find a planet that may or may not be hospitable to life? That may or may not even exist? At least I know for sure where I'm going."

"I meant to stay here. With me. We can care for each other until the end."

A hard stone formed in the place where Zat's heart beat in his chest. He hated to leave his uncle. He was the last remaining member of his family on Earth. Zat's three older brothers left years ago, the early scouts. There had been no good news, barely any news at all. And then his parents and younger sister left to follow in his brothers' path. That was the hardest thing he'd ever had to do, to say goodbye to them. But this would be worse. His uncle had always watched out for Zat—being childless, he was almost like a father. Leaving him felt like the ultimate betrayal.

But he had a dream so beautiful it caused him physical

pain whenever he allowed himself to think of it. He would settle for just a dream, if you could even call it settling. It was everything to Zat. Everything.

Before he could answer, he heard the tell-tale deep breaths of sleep and knew his uncle was gone once more. A life like this? It wasn't a life, it was just preserving the last reserves of energy and fuel until they were both gone for good. Then once the roaches and vipers were done with their flesh, their bones would wither and turn to dust under the blazing orange sun.

And then he thought about the girl again.

And her inexplicable hair.

BABE'S BLOG

WHAT IT'S LIKE TO MOVE AWAY FROM EVERYTHING
YOU KNOW TO A FREAKING ALIEN LANDSCAPE . . .

I envy you, the girl who's lived her entire life in one place. Maybe you were born there, went to school there. Your friends lived on streets with the same names, and saw the same sunsets. Smelled the same flowers. Listened to the same birdsongs. The people in your community shared triumphs and tragedies. School mascots. Even flu epidemics. One day you'll fall in love with someone who knows what makes your heart sing, what makes you burst with pride or collapse in shame. Your memories will be his and his will be yours.

I've lived in your towns and cities. Sometimes for six months. Sometimes for three years. Once, only for two weeks. I've lived in Washington, Oregon, Nevada, Arizona, New Mexico and three different cities in California. I've been on the fringes of your social circles, envying you from a distance. Sometimes you let me in for a better view. Usually, I only get a glimpse.

Here's what I have that you don't. The ability to adapt to whatever fate throws at me. A pretty decent bullshit detector when I meet someone new. Superior powers of observation from always being on the outside looking in. An outsider's appreciation for the so-called disposable people.

Each time my family moves to a new place, we all hit the ground running. Invisible while we check out the new surroundings, and then quickly moving to fit in where we can. Being the youngest of three children, eventually it was just me and my parents—my two older brothers having peeled off along the way, left behind in college towns to shape their own lives.

Yesterday, I arrived in Sugar Dunes, Florida—a sleepy little town in Northwestern Florida, the part of Florida they call the panhandle because . . . well, because it's shaped like the handle of a pan, even though the rest of Florida isn't shaped like a pan at all. As for why they call it a sleepy town, I'm not really sure. People probably don't sleep more than usual here, but Dad says they move at a much slower pace than what we're used to. Maybe it's the awful heat and humidity during the summer, and *Hello!* it's summer. Maybe it's the white sandy beaches and clear turquoise water that SugarDunes.org claims will "tempt you like a siren's song."

Come to me.

Forget about your troubles and ambitions.

Brown yourself under my golden sun.

Comments:
Sweetness: hey i just stumbled on this and its really

good but i feel kinda bad for you so let me know what happens next ☺

Babe: Don't ever feel bad for me.

Sweetness: also this is a really strange blog, you know what i mean? like, most blogs aren't like this.

Babe: It's really more like a diary that I'm sharing. Maybe a bad idea so I'll see how it goes.

Sweetness: no, it's cool don't get me wrong. i like to read peoples' diarys

One

When I heard we were moving to Florida, I was a little excited once I got over the initial disappointment. I'm not exactly a beach person, to the extent that I cover up with long-sleeved shirts and hats and usually head for the closest shade umbrella to protect my lily-white skin. But I like the salty smell and thumping sound of waves as much as the next person. I love the *idea* of a beach, if not the actual beach. There's an excitement that has everything to do with it being the end of land and the mystery of what's on the opposite side.

In my mind, I envisioned South Beach in Miami—a billion-dollar strip of sand, crawling with tourists from all over the world. A paradise for shoppers, partygoers, and people watchers. And who doesn't like to watch people? I like it as much as anyone else.

Unfortunately, what I didn't envision was the Redneck Riviera, which is a derogatory name for what the people here prefer to call the Emerald Coast. I didn't know the panhandle of Florida is more like Alabama than Florida—very much the Deep South. The language spoken here is Deep Southern. And that was a pretty good sign I was doomed to be an outsider once again, since I didn't have a clue how to speak it.

The day after my school year ended, my mom and I hopped on an eastward bound plane. The flight from California took all day with a couple of plane transfers and a long layover in the Atlanta airport. Each time we transferred, our planes got smaller and smaller until we finally squeezed into a thirty seat propeller plane, which was so noisy we had to yell at each other just to be heard. When we landed in the Sugar Dunes Airport late that night, all I could think about was getting to our new house and climbing into bed.

It was just barely into the month of June and already past midnight, so I wasn't prepared for the blast of wet hot that hit me as soon as the flight attendant wrestled open the exit door. I'd worked on my hair before we left in order to make a sleek and shiny first impression in my new hometown, but it was hopeless. As soon as I got off the plane, my hair twisted and frizzed until I looked like Medusa, and if you don't know who she is, let's just say she had snakes for hair.

Lesson One. I had to give up on my Emma Stone dreams and accept the Ronald McDonald look. Either that or shave my head.

Inside the airport terminal, the temperature was sub-freezing.

Lesson Two. People in this part of the country liked it cold. *Really* cold. Except when they were outside and it was really hot. So my hypothalamus, which I didn't even know I had until then and which, by the way, is that little gizmo in your brain that regulates your body temperature among other things, was destined for a state of constant confusion.

"There's your dad!" Mom grabbed me by the arm and pointed straight ahead past the security checkpoint. It'd been a month since we'd seen him and her fast walk turned into a trot and then a full-out run as she dragged her rolling carry-on bag behind her. I did my best to keep up.

Mom and Dad fell into each other's arms, hugging and kissing like long-lost lovers, (which technically they were) and which would've been totally embarrassing if I actually knew anyone within a radius of 2,000 miles, but since I didn't . . . let the good times roll, for all I care. I gave them a moment of privacy before inserting myself into their zone of love.

"Babe!" Dad finally came up for air. "You look fantastic!" (I didn't.) "I've missed you so much." (Okay, I actually missed him too.) "Let's go pick up your luggage and then get you two home."

Mental—no *actual*—*fist pump!*

Home. It sounded so nice.

Since it was dark, I couldn't see much of Sugar Dunes,

but I could smell the pine trees. Yep. Pine trees when I was expecting palm trees. At that point I was still hoping for Miami Beach, and the salty beach smell was unmistakable. But when we finally got our bags and loaded up the truck and started driving, all that was visible for miles and miles on either side of the two-lane highway were the dark silhouettes of a pine forest and the brightest night sky I'd ever seen. The highway was buffered by a strip of palmetto shrubs, and it seemed like we'd been driving forever when it finally spit us out onto a sand and gravel road. A beat-up, lopsided street sign that said *Trout Lane* didn't sound too promising. I had to live on a street named after a fish? Dad turned the truck into a driveway where the mailbox was marked "22." As far as I could tell, there weren't any other houses on this street, so I wasn't sure why we were 22 instead of one or maybe even 1000. But there it was, 22 Trout Lane.

Welcome home again, Babe.

Zat

There was no use pretending he was going back to sleep. Pretending for who? Uncle was unreachable and who knew when he'd wake again? Uncle was a perfect physical specimen, barely in need of nutrients or water, and able to sleep most of the time. By comparison, Zat was ashamed. His overly active thoughts and imagination kept him awake for hours at a time, boosting his metabolic rate and demanding a caloric intake which could sustain three ordinary citizens.

Zat was hungry. And thirsty, too. He pressed his fingertips against his eyeballs until they ached. Finally, he rose up on legs weak from disuse. He slipped through the solar door which reconstructed its cells in his wake. His home, like all the others for as far as he could see, was black and cubical in shape. Razor-thin solar cells kept the insides of these homes cool and bright. Most were unoccupied now, abandoned as their former owners sought the safety of new worlds far from this doomed planet.

Earth. Zat knew it had once been green and covered with enormous bodies of water, blue to the eye when observed from far off in space. Earth, in its infancy, was a beautiful sight to behold. But now, in its old age, drawing ever closer to the expanding sun, it was hideous. Hostile. Beautiful only in the collective memory of the human species.

Outside, there was still enough light to guide Zat to the community center. It was better that way, although the heat was barely tolerable. The vipers didn't come out until late at night. They were harder to spot in the dark, even with the powerful beam of his light stick. And to die from the venom of a viper attack before he ever had the chance to . . . that was an irony he wouldn't allow himself to consider.

He stooped to snap a small limb from the juicy cactus plant, and he sucked noisily until the only thing left was the dried outer skin which he dropped on the ground. There was powdered beetle meal at home. He'd have some later when Uncle was asleep and couldn't scold him for staying awake so long. He'd prepare a hefty supply of the meal for Uncle before he left for good. Enough maybe to last him until the end. But Uncle would find someone after Zat was gone. He'd make a new alliance with one of the others who chose to stay behind.

The gargantuan sun seemed to melt the edge of the horizon as it slowly descended from sight. Zat was glad to be out of the house. Better to deal with the rude questions of those still preparing to leave. Saying their goodbyes at the community center. Trading rumors and theories of what was in store for them. Better to do that than to be alone with his thoughts for one more second.

Sahra might be there, but he hoped not. No one could understand why Zat refused the chance to match with her. He was old enough, and they'd both been entered into the lottery, but Zat withdrew before it was held. He knew Sahra would match with him; her father would make sure of it. But he couldn't go through with it because it wasn't honest. It would have been unfair to Sahra. His heart could never settle with her.

She was astonished when he first told her of his decision. They wouldn't be leaving together with his family. Or her family. He had his own dreams. Others had done it successfully, he trusted. Maybe there would be more news this very day from Pioneer One, the first to forge the path Zat soon hoped to follow. If there was any news he'd hear it first at the community center. Maybe a bit of information that would calm his last-minute jitters.

But jitters or not, this was his decision. *Zat is a dreamer,* he'd heard the others snickering behind his back. *He's spent too much time in the sun. He can't think logically anymore. Heading straight to a certain death.* People didn't dream anymore. Thankfully, they did in the early times when the Earth was still a wondrous thing that humans wrote about with as much love as they felt for another person.

What a wonderful thing it is to dream. To live out random and fantastical experiences every night. He knew dreams could be terrifying, but he also knew they could be magical.

    The red-headed girl, Babe. What did she dream about? He couldn't wait to find out.

BABE'S BLOG

I came all the way from California with its much higher energy level and much denser population. In California I had (have) a boyfriend, Perry, who seemed to instantly appreciate me and managed to fall in love with me in just a few short weeks. We both like to write and . . . well, we both like to write. We were inseparable, until we were separated last week, just two days after my seventeenth birthday.

Dad left first in order to get started at his new job and prepare a home for Mom and me. Thankfully, I was allowed to stay behind to finish up my junior year of high school in California. I was sad but not heart-broken to say goodbye to Perry. After all, adaptability is one of my strengths and I knew that in one year I could choose my own future and plant my roots wherever I decided to plant them, just like my older brothers. Perry and I were going to apply to the same colleges and Skype with each other every night during our year apart. A short trip back to California wasn't out of the question, according to my parents, who obviously felt extreme guilt for the transient life they'd forced me to live. It wasn't the end of the world.

Or was it?

I suppose I should mention that my father's a golf pro. My life has been an endless parade of country clubs at a time when golf and country clubs are almost a relic from the past. In this economy, golf is once again becoming the elitist sport it used to be. The price of a golf membership at some country clubs is equal to the cost of buying a home, which is why we never stay long in any one place. Costs are up, incomes are down, and golf pros like my dad have to go wherever they can find work.

My name is Babe, after Babe Didrikson Zaharias. I usually don't bother to explain this to people because nobody my age has ever heard of her, even though she was one of the greatest women golfers ever. My parents, who met on the golf team of their college, thought it would be the perfect name for their only daughter. Their two sons, my older brothers, are both scratch golfers who play for their colleges. Their names are Arnold and Jack.

Me, tennis is my game. I'm pretty good at it, but I'm honored to be named after Babe Zaharias. She was tough and fearless and paved the way for other women to succeed in a world of men. I must admit, I've had to put up with a fair amount of teasing because of my name, but I've never regretted it, not even once.

Comments:

Sweetness: hey it's me again and this is totally sad *crying* but i thin its really cool that youre named after soemone whos so strong

    Babe: Thanks, but I wish you wouldn't think my life is so sad because it's not.

        Sweetness: im telling all my friends about ur blog and i just wanted to say that i totally know someone on facebook who lives in cali and his name is perry and was wondering if thats ur bf

            Babe: I doubt it's the same guy but I'm not going to say his last name because it wouldn't be cool.

                Sweetness: oh ya i know that but i was still wondering

Sandman: Babe! haha. r u a babe?

    Babe: No comment.

Two

Every house I'd ever lived in had been a version of the same basic floor plan. Enter in the front door. To your right are three bedrooms lined up in a row. Straight in front of you is a living/dining area. To the left is the kitchen. Bathrooms are sprinkled in.

There were minor differences. Sometimes the bedrooms were to the left and the kitchen to the right. And occasionally a family room extended from the dining room. But I pretty much always knew what the house would look like before I ever stepped foot inside.

We were always renters and this time was no different. When you can't be sure how long your job will last, you can't commit to buying a house. And even if we wanted to buy, my family was always short of cash. Money was even tighter because my parents tried to help my brothers out with some of their college costs, as much as they could.

"I tried to fix things up nice for you," Dad said apologetically. "But there are a few problems that still need taking care of."

I immediately knew what one of those problems was when I walked through the door. Fans were blowing air from every corner of every room and still it felt like I was soaking in a hot tub. A disturbingly moldy smell made me nauseous, like when you throw a wet towel in the dirty laundry hamper and then discover it a week later. Still wet and still dirty.

"We're here now and I don't start work until next week," Mom said brightly. "We'll get everything straightened out, won't we, Baby?" My mom calls me Baby. *Waaah!*

"Apart from the obvious air conditioner malfunction," my dad went on, "I'm sorry to say I'm also having issues with the Wi-Fi and cable."

"What kind of issues?" Air conditioning was one thing. Wi-Fi and cable was non-negotiable. But my dad was notoriously tech-ignorant so I didn't immediately panic. I was pretty handy at tweaking routers and modems after so many moves.

"They claimed everything was set up, but I can't get anything to work. I called them, and they put us back on the bottom of the waiting list. Next week." My dad looked at me sheepishly. "Sorry."

I felt bad for my dad. He never lost the optimism that each new move would be the final one. The one we'd fall in love with and the job would be permanent and secure and we'd never move again. He wanted us to believe it too, but I'd had too many letdowns to buy into that. A busted air conditioner with no Wi-Fi or cable wasn't exactly a promising start to our latest move. But you couldn't move around as much as we did and survive if you were a whiner. That much, at least, I'd learned.

So much for Skyping with Perry if I couldn't fix it myself. I would've texted him but I'd already tried my cell phone and we were out of the service area. Just great. In the middle of a pine forest on a street named after a fish, and I couldn't even send a text.

"Good news though, honey. You have a job in the tennis shop. Booking courts and lessons, ringing up purchases. Should be fun."

Okay, it was kind of good news because I needed the money and I liked to stay busy. Sitting around the house all day, communing with whatever nature was outside our door wasn't exactly part of my plan. Mom would be working in the golf shop and this was the life we were used to. "When do I start?"

"Next week. You and Mom settle in first. The moving truck comes Thursday."

I didn't even know what day it was when I finally lay my head down on my pillow. The cross-country trip seemed more like a month than a day. And Sugar Dunes, Florida was a whole different universe than California. I didn't think it was possible to keep my eyes open for more than a few seconds in spite of the noisy whirr of the fan . . . and the sheen of sweat which was beginning to feel like a second skin . . . and the barking tree frogs just outside my window . . . and the dip in the middle of my musty old mattress . . . and my parents' muffled voices coming from the other side of the paper thin bedroom wall.

At some point, the switch in my mind simply turned off all those new sounds and smells, and I finally fell asleep. At some point I dreamed I was walking on a beach of sugar-white sand. I walked by a small open-air café with tables protected from the sun by brightly striped umbrellas.

When I woke the next morning, I sat straight up in bed gulping for air. For a few seconds it felt like I was underwater breathing in pure liquid, my lungs shriveled to a fraction of their normal capacity by the overbearing heat. I had a fierce pain in my forehead that went away after a few minutes of sitting up.

I looked around my room and could tell Dad had tried to make it comfortable for me. I'd fallen asleep on top of the bed cover, a patterned pink thing he probably picked up in a thrift shop. I loved him for doing it even if I didn't love the cover itself. In fact, an exact replica of its pattern was on my arm, and if I looked in the mirror I'd probably see it on my cheek too. There was a small bedside table with a green plastic vase which held two gorgeous, pink, exotic-looking flowers. On the wall above my bed, he'd hung an artistically staged and framed photo. Maybe it came with the house, or maybe he picked it up at the same place he got my bedspread and the green vase.

I stared at the picture and for some reason it reminded me of something. After a minute I realized I'd dreamed of this place. The small café set on the white sand beach peeking out from between the dunes. A few outdoor tables capped by big umbrellas striped in bright shades of yellow and green.

Maybe I'd seen the picture without even being aware of it when I came to bed, but there was no light fixture in my room and it'd been dark. There'd be a floor lamp I could use when the moving truck came with our stuff. In the meantime, I needed to switch bedrooms. My parents and I honestly needed a sound barrier between us with those paper-thin walls.

I heard a noise outside my window so I jumped up to investigate. Right outside my curtainless window was an older man. At least he looked old, but it's possible he was just sun-fried. He was wearing a gray one-piece jumpsuit with an identification tag sewed under his right shoulder. He held a metal wand attached to a thin hose, which was attached to a dented metal canister.

"Mornin' miss!" he called out, loud enough that I could hear him through the glass. Man, did I ever need to get some curtains up fast. Thank goodness I'd fallen asleep with all my clothes on.

I pried open the swollen, wood-framed window.

"Hello." I read the tag on his coveralls—"Kill-em-Dead Roach & Pest Control."

"Sorry to have disturbed yew. I'll be outta here in just a few minutes."

"No problem," I said, all cool even though it was kind of a problem. Or at least a literal rude awakening.

"Any areas that require special attention today?" he asked. By special attention I figured he meant extra poison or whatever it was he was carrying around inside the canister.

"My mom and I just got here last night, so I guess do whatever you usually do."

"Alright then, miss . . .?"

"Babe," I offered.

"Miss Babe." He was spraying the ground right up against the house. "Got yourself a fire ant nest over here. I'll take care of it for yew, but avoid the area for a while."

Fire ant? What kind of strange creature was that?

My mom was in the kitchen frying up bacon and eggs. "Sorry, Baby, this is all Dad had in the refrigerator. There's some milk if you want cereal instead."

I opened the refrigerator and found a few pathetic looking apples which yielded to the pressure of my finger when I pushed lightly. Also, a plastic bag of carrots that had never been opened—Dad's attempt to honor my vegetarianism.

"I'll have some eggs if you have extra." I sat down at the kitchen table and made the best of one of the apples. "There's a man spraying for bugs out back."

"His name's Billy. Dad told me he comes with the house. I called the air conditioner repair guy and begged him to come out today. He promised he would."

"Do we have a car?" I wanted to get out and see what life was like outside of Trout Lane which, to be honest, wasn't very exciting so far.

"Your father had to take the truck to work, but he said you can use the bike in the garage if you want to explore.

If you really want the truck, I suppose you could ride over to the club and pick it up."

"How far away is the club?"

"Oh, I don't know. I don't think it's too far. We can ask Billy if he's still around."

"I'll go check. And Mom . . . I think I need to move into the other bedroom. Too close to yours, and those walls aren't very soundproof."

My mom turned beet red. "What do you mean? What exactly did you hear?"

"Eeew! I just heard you talking, but thanks for the gross image I'll never get out of my mind. Can you help me move the bed later on?"

"Happy to oblige." My mom smiled apologetically. "And Babe? Cable and Wi-Fi are working just fine. I don't know what your father was talking about."

"Oh great! Now if we only had cell phone reception."

"That's working just fine too. At least, mine is. Check yours."

I flipped my phone open and saw about a hundred texts that had come in from Perry during the night.

What the . . .?

This day was looking better and better.

Billy was just about ready to leave when I caught up with him to ask for directions to the club where Dad worked and where Mom and I would be working soon.

"It's just down the road a bit. Go back out to the main road and turn right . . . when you see the Piggly Wiggly, make a left and keep going. Cain't miss it."

"Piggly wiggly?" Was this another strange creature like the fire ant, which in my imagination was a tiny fire-breathing dragon?

"That's right. Make a left just before the Piggly Wiggly. Cain't miss it."

"Is it far?"

Billy considered this for a moment before answering. "No, it's not too far. You have a nice day, you hear? I'll be back next week."

Next week? Did creatures multiply that quickly around here? It seemed to me he'd laid down enough poison to stifle a thousand generations of bugs.

ZAT

The community center, just a larger version of every other structure, was sparsely filled. When Zat was young, the center drew crowds wanting to exchange ideas, to make matches, to talk about what their future might look like. That was before the first scouts left. In the intervening years, most had already abandoned the planet, some traveling only as far as the temporary, less desirable planets. Others forged ahead with the hope of discovering a new world. A new Earth, the way it once was.

The moment Zat walked in, he regretted his decision to go there. It was good to be around people his own age but he would always be the outsider. He was the one choosing the road less traveled, even though it would be months, possibly years, before his turn came up. Most of the new technology was directed toward space travel. Very little had been invested in time travel. Time travel was an older technology, all but abandoned. The equipment that still existed was outdated and only able to handle a few at a time. Anyone still interested in that option was forced to wait their turn based on age. Older pioneers first.

Since Pioneer One made the first journey back in time, few were interested in following. The government claimed he was able to send signals before going dark. But when no other signals were forthcoming, people lost hope and the government turned its resources back to space travel. Most thought Pioneer One was dead, but Zat didn't. Zat and the other believers were convinced that Pioneer One was in the place by that wondrous body of water, inhabiting the mind of a brilliant scholar who'd left the world of academia to spend his older years playing games (another quirk of ancient humans) and pulling fish from the sea to be eaten and enjoyed for their nutrients and taste.

Yet knowing how way leads onto way,
I doubted if I should ever come back.

Why didn't people write poetry anymore? Another art lost to time. So much was lost and yet Zat was constantly being accused of romanticizing the past where humans fought against each other and passed microbes into each other's bodies that sickened and even killed. Zat would give anything to swim in an ocean. Sit under the shade of a tree. A real tree. The petrified forest he once saw as a child was just a ghost of what had once blanketed the earth.

"Zat."

Sahra surprised him from behind. He turned quickly

to see her face, at once sad and beautiful. He was sorry for what he wished could have been but never was.

"Sahra. I thought I'd see you here."

"How is your uncle?"

"Very well. He sleeps most of the time now. I thought I'd come see how everyone was doing."

"You know we're leaving soon."

"I know. Uncle told me."

"It's not too late, Zat. To come with us. Father would arrange it."

"And I appreciate it, Sahra, believe me I do. I'm not even worthy of your offer—"

"That's silly, Zat. Of course you're worthy."

"—but you know I've made up my mind."

Sahra looked down at the ground. She seemed to be a source of infinite sadness but Zat knew it really emanated from him. Life had never been easy and there was no reason why it should start now.

"You're still going to that place? By the ocean?" Sahra's eyes were black and unreadable.

"It's my arranged destination. It's been coded and cleared. Now I'm just waiting."

"It doesn't seem wrong to you? To take over a person's thoughts? Their minds?"

"It's not really their thoughts. It's a subconscious period where the thoughts aren't directed in a rational manner. They're aimless meanderings. It happens when they sleep."

"I know what a dream is, Zat."

"I know you know. I just wanted to make it clear I wasn't taking over anyone's mind."

"Well, that's the way it seems to me. And so pointless when there's no proof of success. Why not just stay here with your uncle if you're determined to die?"

They stood facing each other, an island of discord in the small sea of mingling youth.

"Sahra. If we shan't see each other ever again, let's not part like this. Let our last words be ones of love and kindness."

"I know. I'm sorry. It's just . . . who have you chosen as your destination? A scientist? A futurist?"

Zat thought again of the girl with the red hair. He thought of her clear, light skin that looked as though it would feel almost gelatinous. What *would* it feel like to run his finger down the length of her arm? Her leg? Through her hair?

"Just a person. A regular person with no special talent beyond a forceful yet curious temperament. Adaptable, so perhaps I'll be more readily accepted."

He knew the girl, Babe, would just be arriving in that place near the ocean at his programmed time. The Gulf of Mexico, as it was called back then, was now just an unnamed dry desert bed. She didn't dream of it yet because she had never seen it. But she would. She would very soon. And when she did, he hoped he'd be there with her if everything went the way it should.

"I hope for your sake he accepts you. I hope you don't live to regret your decision . . . or worse." Sahra looked away and took a sudden sharp breath as if to tamp down her sorrow. "How old is he?" she asked.

He. Zat decided not to enlighten Sahra about the sex of his future host. Why drive another wedge between them when this was most likely the last conversation they'd ever have?

"The same as us. I thought it was best so I could experience age-relevant events."

Maybe he should go home. He'd probably made a mistake by coming tonight.

BABE'S BLOG

CHECKING OUT THE NEW SURROUNDINGS . . .

The bike in the garage is promising. A rusty old green thing that looks like it might have been new when my mom was a kid. It has a basket, which is dorky but useful. I test it out in the driveway. Tires pumped and in good condition (thanks, Dad). No gears but, hey, no hills, so that's a wash. An old-fashioned rusty bell that actually works. A clear drop of oil leaking from the bell onto my thumb is a hint Dad's been working on the bike in preparation for my arrival.

In spite of the stifling heat, I dress in a long-sleeved blue cotton shirt and cut-offs (my white legs slathered with sunscreen). My crazy hair is stuffed into a wide-brimmed canvas hat—the kind you'd expect to see on an African safari. With my round, over-sized sunglasses completing the look, I'm sure I look slightly . . . unusual. I pack four water bottles into the basket along with my backpack and set off for my first adventure.

The smooth cement of our driveway gives way to the sand and gravel crunch of Trout Lane. I pause to check out my new street but can see nothing much of interest besides our house. Just a lot of sandy looking soil and some tall pines. Makes me wonder where all those noisy tree frogs went, the ones that kept me awake last night.

I ride back out to the main road that delivered us here last night. At last I can see it for what it is, a highway without any street lights. And without any cars.

Then a truck whizzes by and honks. I'm not sure if I'm doing something wrong or if he's just being friendly. There isn't a bike lane so I stay as far to the right as I can without falling off the pavement.

After about five minutes of pedaling, another car speeds by and I realize I'm already thirsty. I get off my bike and guide it from the road into an area that looks to be free of fire ant nests, even though I'm not exactly sure what a fire ant nest might look like. I down an entire bottle of water in less than thirty seconds. That happened after only five minutes? I maybe should've brought more water.

Back on my bike and back on the road, I pedal on. Another few minutes and another car passes. The sun's so hot it emits a high frequency note like a chorus of a million hysterical crickets. Even though my shirt sticks to me like a wet rag, I resist the urge to pull over for another drink.

Peering off in the distance I see wavy lines of heat rising from the blacktop, nothing that looks like a piggly wiggly, or anything else for that matter. Nothing but pine trees and the occasional car that passes every five minutes or so. It occurs to me I might die from the heat out in the middle of nowhere. But I'm not about to turn around and go home. I'm on a mission and I've chosen to accept it. Mission impossible? I hope not.

Another ten minutes and my doubts turn serious. Not even one car comes by during that time. I get off my bike again and gulp down a second bottle of water. My body's expelling water through sweat faster than I can drink it. My face feels like the color it probably is. Red. Or possibly purple. Finally, a white pick-up truck traveling in the opposite direction pulls off to the side of the road—"Cummings' Emergency AC Repair," emblazoned on the driver's door. I can definitely appreciate the fact that a broken air conditioner is an emergency around here. The driver's side window rolls down.

"Are you alright?" A friendly-faced woman with glowing brown skin and French-braided hair looks out at me with . . . alarm?

"I'm fine, thank you." Pretty embarrassing to know a passerby in a moving vehicle thinks I look like I might need 9-1-1.

"Are you sure I can't give you a lift somewhere?"

"Oh no," I laugh with false bravado as though this ride is a daily and pleasurable event in my life. But panic starts to set in as the window slides back up. "Excuse me please!" The window goes back down. "Could you tell me how far a piggly wiggly is up ahead?" I hope with all my heart she knows what I'm talking about.

"It's about a mile up the road. Is that where you're going?"

"Yes," I lie. If I tell her I'm going even further, I think she'll call someone to lock me up. "I heard it wasn't far."

"It's not far if you're driving," the friendly lady says, "but it's pretty hot to be out here on a bike. We can put your bike in the back of my truck and I could take you there."

But my independence (or is it stubbornness?) won't allow me to accept her offer. Scratch that. I think it's plain old embarrassment.

"Oh, just a mile? No, I'll be fine but thanks for the offer."

"Alright then," she looks doubtful. "Have a nice day."

"Same to you!" I use my most cheerful voice while doing a quick estimate of how many minutes it will take to travel the half mile before I could stop for my next bottle of water. There has to be some kind of relief at this "piggly wiggly," or at least I hope so.

The Piggly Wiggly turns out to be nothing more than a big supermarket. It's out there in the middle of what appears to be nowhere, but probably is somewhere. There's nothing else in sight, just a huge concrete building surrounded by a huge blacktop parking lot which could fit a thousand cars, but only has about twenty. Seeing no bike rack, and having no kickstand, I lean my trusty transportation against the wall of the shopping cart corral. No bike lock—I didn't think I'd be stopping anywhere on the way so it hadn't occurred to me to look for one. But I take a leap of faith and decide this bicycle isn't going to be a magnet for a bicycle thief.

I can't wait to get inside and even the shocking temperature differential doesn't bother me this time; in fact, I love it. I feel the redness of heat drain from my cheeks as I wander through the aisles, eventually picking up another four bottles of water.

"Can you tell me how far the Crystal Point Resort is?" I ask the cashier who looks like she's only a few years older than me.

"Oh, it's not far," she smiles at me. "Just down the road a bit."

By now I know enough not to trust the term *a bit*. Should I let her know I'm on bike and then ask the question again? Maybe *a bit* would mean something different in that case. But I decide to go with it. I've come too far to turn back, so what does it matter?

"Visiting?" she asks.

"No, I just moved here."

"Oh, I thought . . ." she hands me change for my twenty-dollar bill.

She doesn't have to finish the sentence. I know what she thought. My clothes are strange and I have no trace of a southern accent. I don't look like anyone else in the store.

"Have a great day!" she chirps.

People are nice here, but will I ever belong? Can I?

Comments:

Sandman: Sweetness r u here? never mind
Sweetness: haha you dont know what a piggly wiggly is? and also your diary is strange the way you write it like its happening right now. my diary is totally different than this but i still like yours too.
Babe: Thanks?

THREE

Finally, a little bit really was a little bit, and just in time. With my first glimpse of the golf course greens, the sky turned dark with monstrous black clouds that appeared out of nowhere, ominously bumping up against each other to blot out the sun.

When the first fat raindrops splashed against my back, it felt good. The temperature didn't drop much, but at least the sun was temporarily neutralized.

A few minutes later, I got my first introduction to a Florida summer storm. With no advance warning, and before my mind could process what was happening, the storm illustrated the meaning of the phrase *force of nature*. Water was basically dumped from the sky. In California, it never rained during the summer, and when it did rain, it never fell with that intensity.

Puddles turned into ponds in front of my eyes. The thunder was earsplitting. Golden daggers of lightning cut through the sky. I knew enough to know I should be scared, out in the open totally unprotected and sitting on a metal bicycle. But the rush of being in the middle of a show like that . . . I had to talk some sense into myself to hurry up and get out of it.

I pedaled furiously toward the columns that marked the entrance of Crystal Point Yacht and Country Club. A small uniformed man in the guard house motioned me under an eave. And just when my initial excitement was turning into anxiety, the storm stopped. Just like that.

The heavyweight clouds rumbled off like bullies looking for someone new to pick on. The sky was nothing but blue and the sun came out of hiding, hissing like an angry snake. Pools of water disappeared into the ground without a trace.

A few minutes later, I was beginning to doubt the whole thing had ever happened.

"I guess you can be on your way now, ma'am," the small guard said with a nod.

"Actually I'm here to see Pat Fremont. He's my father."

"Pat, the new golf pro?" The guard opened his eyes wide. "You know how to get to the golf shop?"

I shook my head, which resulted in him pulling out a map that looked like one of those placemats they give to kids in the restaurants along with a box of crayons. The guard, who introduced himself as Earl, charted my path with a red marker.

"Not too far," he said. "Just down the road a bit." He looked at me somewhat skeptically. I must have been a sorry sight by then even though my clothes were already dry from the soaking they'd just received. "I can call security to take you there. Put your bike in the back of one of our trucks."

I'd come this far and wasn't about to give up. "I'll be okay. Thanks, Earl."

"You're a tough one, airnch you?" It was sort of a cross between aren't and ain't. "What's your name?"

"Babe." I waited for the reaction I was sure would come. I could never introduce myself without some feedback about my name.

"Babe, wait just a second if you don't mind." Earl bent over and rummaged around under the counter of the guard house.

When he straightened up he was holding a camera. "Mind if I take a picture? I'm kind of a shutterbug . . . hobby of mine."

Well, the truth was I did mind a bit but our family had befriended a lot of Earls over the years. The men and women who spent their lives in the tiny guard houses of resorts across the country. They were people who could make your life easier. They'd guide you to the best and cheapest restaurants, accept packages for you when you couldn't be home, pull strings to get the cable guy out to your house faster, give you the lowdown on the club members—who to avoid and who you could count on for the big Christmas tips. Guys like Earl played an important role, so you never wanted to alienate them if you could help it

"Not at all," I said, straddling my ancient bike and turning to face the camera with my cheesiest Hollywood smile.

I followed the map to the marina. Once there, I had the option to continue riding on the street or taking the narrow boardwalk where yachts—which cost more than most people make in a lifetime—were tied to docks with strong, thick ropes. The boardwalk seemed much more interesting, but the wide gaps between slats of wood made it impossible for me to ride. I got off my bike and pushed it along the boardwalk while checking out boats that looked more like mansions than sea-going vessels.

Crews were busy on most of the boats, scrubbing decks, hosing down the sides, vacuuming. I knew a yacht was always kept ready for the whim of its owner and it took a lot of work from a lot of people to keep them that way. I'd seen them before on another coast with other names. The crews, mostly young men, were part of my world—the people who made things run smoothly for the pleasure of the super-rich. We needed the jobs that paid for our food and rent, and put clothes on our backs. For those lucky enough to play inside the gates of the Crystal Point Yacht and Country Club, the rest of us were just background noise. But most of us knew the truth about what little happiness those expensive toys actually delivered. We didn't desire them—what good would that do? That lifestyle was a lottery not many people were lucky enough to win.

When the marina came to an end, I climbed back on my bike and continued on the main road which ran through Crystal Point, connecting its waterfront custom homes to all points of pleasure, wrapping them together with a silky black bow. The marina gave way to red clay tennis courts and Olympic sized pools. Velvety green acres of fairways lined the road on either side. I saw the main clubhouse with its white stucco walls and turquoise tiled roof. Just across the parking lot was a much smaller, but similarly styled building: the golf clubhouse. That would be Dad's kingdom for as long as he could hold on to his job.

"Babe, honey! How'd you get here?" Apparently Mom hadn't called ahead to prepare him, but my generally messy appearance must have given him a clue as to how I got there.

"I rode the bike."

"All the way here? What a champ!" I could tell he was proud of me. Many parents might have been horrified.

"Yup. Thought I'd come get the truck and explore the town."

"I'm just about to go out for a lesson, but here's the key. Make sure you're here to pick me up by six and we'll throw the bike in the back of the truck."

Lucky for me, I could drive a stick shift. The truck's air conditioner didn't exactly churn out cold air, but at least it was coolish.

On my way out the gate, I saw Earl and remembered that Mom had asked me to pick up some fish for dinner.

"That seems a more sensible way to travel." He smiled

approvingly at the truck.

"I was just wondering, Earl, where's a good place to buy fresh fish?"

"Nuggins is the best," he offered without hesitation.

"Nuggins . . . like N-U-G-G-I-N-S?"

"Nah. It's Vietnamese. N-G-U-Y-E-N apostrophe S. Nuggins."

I didn't know how to pronounce it myself, but I was pretty sure it wasn't Nuggins. Earl gave me some directions about it being just down the road a bit, not far, you make a left here and a right there, something about a bridge, and you can't miss it.

Then just as I was about to thank him and go off in search of Nuggins or whatever it was, Earl slapped his forehead like he'd just remembered something.

"Your cable and internet workin' okay now?"

"Yeah," I said wondering how he already knew about it. But then again, my dad had probably mentioned something earlier. "It's working fine now. For some reason it wasn't working last night."

"I called a guy I know at the cable company. There's a lot they can do remotely."

"Thanks, I owe you big time."

"Now you go have yourself a great day, you hear? And welcome to Sugar Dunes, home of the whitest beaches and bluest water you'll ever see in ten lifetimes!"

He was right about that.

I finally found Nguyen's Fish Market and at the same time confirmed once again that *a bit* could really mean *a bit* around here or it could mean *a lot*. In this case it was a lot. A lot of miles away, that is. Turns out it was completely on the other side of the Bay from where we lived, in an area which could best be described as humble. Small, gray buildings that had been beaten up by the moist, salty air for so many years were separated by wide gravel parking lots—one sad building looking just like the other. I was struck by the open space out here. Nobody was fighting for parking places in Sugar Dunes. Parking places were fighting for cars.

Nguyen's, on the other hand, was jammed. I squeezed the truck into a narrow spot between two other trucks and went in to have a look. I didn't know one type of fish from another but I suspected everything there was fresh off the boats.

The customers inside waited in two lines. In the first line you gave your order to a guy (an Asian man about my dad's age), and he wrapped it in white paper, weighed it, wrote a price on it, and handed it to you over the counter. After that you went to the second line where an Asian woman with a thick accent (probably the wife) rang up your purchase. There were so many people in the close space that, in spite of the fans blowing back and forth, the humidity and sight of all the dead fish made me queasy.

I walked back and forth staring at beds of ice chips where shrimp, flounder, grouper, snapper, catfish, and blue crabs competed for my attention like puppies in a pet store. How was a fish novice like me supposed to decide? I noticed a girl behind the counter sitting at a small card table sketching on a sheet of the white paper used for wrapping fish—an ink drawing of an exotic-looking bird, tail feathers draped over the branch of a small tree. It was beautifully drawn; I could tell even from that distance.

When I caught her eye, she put down the black ink pen she was holding and came to the front to help me. She was around my age but smaller, far more delicate, and beautiful without the aid of makeup. Her black hair was pulled straight off her face into a ponytail. I figured she must be the daughter.

"Can I help you find something?" she asked in a soft southern accent.

"Can you suggest something my mom could make for dinner?"

"The snapper's always good."

I glanced at the carnation pink fillets and decided that being a pescatarian was almost as good as being a vegetarian. Anyway, it was either that or starve to death.

"Could you give me enough to feed three hungry people please, or . . . I guess I should go stand in that other line."

In a flash she'd wrapped and weighed the fillets, and placed them in my hand.

What happened next can only be described as an out-of-body experience. I heard someone call out my name just as a mind-blowing pain started in my left foot and ripped all the way up the back of my leg. It seemed to happen in a split second but it must have been longer because when I came out of it, the girl was staring at me.

"Are you alright?" she asked.

I raised my ankle and rubbed away the memory of pain. Probably a leftover from an old tennis injury of mine—an Achilles tendon tear.

"I'm fine. I guess the heat got to me."

"Do you wanna come in the back and sit down for a minute?"

"No, really, I'm fine. Thanks."

Back in the truck, I blasted the AC right at my face.

Zat

Walking away from the lights and voices of the center, Zat was filled with a deep sense of regret. His would be a lonely journey into an unknown, without family and friends. He wasn't sure what had drawn him there tonight—a last chance to strengthen memories of people he'd grown up with? Memories he could take with him to sustain him for whatever lay ahead? Maybe he was hoping for a shot of courage. Or at least someone to take an interest in him, his choice, his future. That didn't happen.

It was every man and woman for themselves now, and if you weren't part of a person's future, you didn't exist for them anymore. They had no time for you in the most literal sense.

Except Sahra.

But even Sahra didn't understand Zat. She could never

feel what moved his soul. The poetry that spoke to him from a beautiful, messy, chaotic world of long ago. A blue planet shrouded in clouds. A place where people dreamed even when they were awake.

Sahra was practical. Zat was not. They were never meant to be.

He looked ahead and saw a flight of wild ducks etching themselves against the sky over the water, then blurring, then etching again, and he knew no man was ever alone on the sea.

The dry, powdery soil reached Zat's ankles creating clouds so thick in his wake they obscured his legs to the knees. He walked slowly, carefully moving the light stick in front of him from left to right and then back again, dragging it through the dust to expose a viper, if one should be lying in wait. Maybe he should have stayed the night at the community center, but he couldn't bear the isolation. He felt more alone there among the others than he ever felt in his own home. In his own mind.

When the pain tore through his calf, searing the flesh all the way up to his groin, he'd been thinking of Babe, and he called out her name.

The way she gripped a racket in strong, capable hands. Gliding across a red rectangle of clay in pursuit of a small yellow ball in a game they called tennis. Her legs were powerful and she moved with joy and confidence.

She was so alive.

Her mind so blissfully pure.

FOUR

When I pulled into the driveway of my house, the woman who'd offered me a ride earlier in the day was just pulling out. Cummings' Emergency AC Repair.

"Back so soon?" Mom was surprised to see me.

"Hey, Mom, I saw the air conditioner lady earlier today. Why didn't she fix it?" The house was still hot and the fans were still whirring.

"Some part they don't keep in stock. She'll be back tomorrow. Her name's Delores Cummings but she likes to be called Dee. Oh, and Baby . . . it's not all bad news. Dee helped me move your bed into the third bedroom and guess what? You've got your own air conditioning room unit. Dee says the central air vent doesn't reach into that room for whatever reason."

I went to my new bedroom and opened the door. The

room unit was belching out cold air with a fierce rattle guaranteed to drown out any competing noise. I thought regretfully of the barking tree frogs I wouldn't be able to hear at night anymore. But it was cold and cold was good. And there were actual blinds that covered the windows. No more early morning wake-up calls from Billy the bug man.

There was my bed all made up with the pink patterned cover. And there was the side table with the green plastic vase and the gorgeous pink blossoms. I looked around the room imagining my stuff in it—plotting how to make it look like more than the boring cubicle it was. I noticed Mom hadn't moved the framed photograph from the other room which was fine with me since I had my own favorite posters which would be arriving with the moving van. I was already scoping out where they would all go. But my mind kept going back to the picture that somehow inserted itself into my dream. Dad must've put some love into it when he picked it out for me. I couldn't just abandon it to the now empty bedroom that would eventually get turned into an "office"—our family's code word for junk room.

I found a hammer in the garage and re-hung the photo, centered directly over the bed in my new room.

By the time I brought my dad home from work that night, I was a lot more familiar with Sugar Dunes, Florida and the Crystal Point Yacht and Country Club.

After dinner I set up my laptop in my room and Skyped with Perry. Everything seemed almost normal.

Almost like I was back in Cali, sprawled across his bed working on homework together. Almost. But after a while, we both had other things to do. Truth was, I was getting tired. I hadn't slept well the night before, but I was going to have no trouble sleeping tonight.

Zat

Luckily for Zat, it was only a few minutes' walk back to the community center. Luckier still, Sahra was still there. Sahra, whose father could still move mountains to make things happen. Who still exerted influence for the brief remaining time before his family left the dying Earth for good.

Zat's leg was swollen and purple by the time he fell through the threshold, his head falling against his outstretched arm, preventing an even worse injury. The skin split and peeled back to reveal muscles and cords beneath its surface. Zat was delirious, rambling nonsensically about an old man alone in a boat in the middle of an endless blue sea. About a girl with red hair that tumbled from her head.

He would never last the night.

Someone had to give up a coveted spot to leave this ruined Earth in favor of the dreams of a long ago soul. Someone who had possibly been waiting his turn for months. Even years. A few people grumbled this was a waste of resources for a boy who most likely wouldn't survive the journey, let alone the night. A misuse of the transporter which would require another thirty days of recharging before it was ready for the next person. But not many people cared about this program anymore. And Zat was going to die. This day. This hour. This minute.

This was his time, selected by fate.

Unless someone or something intervened.

By the time Zat was placed in the transporter, there were barely enough brain waves to complete the operation. Sahra stayed by his side until he was gone. Until only the shell of his abandoned body remained.

BABE'S BLOG

Have you ever had a dream that seems to go on all night? Maybe it did or maybe it just felt like it did but . . . phew!

THE DREAM . . .

I'm walking along the beach minding my own business and enjoying the day. Picture-perfect, almost cartoonish waves breaking to my right. Dazzling white sand dunes rolling by on my left. In a place where the sand dips between two dunes I see a beachside café with brightly colored sun umbrellas silhouetted against a cloudless blue sky. Someone is sitting by himself at one of the tables, his face hidden in the shadows. I decide to climb up the dune to get a better look but the sand slips from under my bare feet when I try. The more I struggle to climb, the more the sand slides, and I get nowhere. My knees and thigh muscles ache from exertion but still I can't make it. I can give up, go back to the beach and continue my walk, but some inner voice drives me forward. I need to see what's up there. I need to see *who's* up there. And then he's standing above me, reaching down to offer his hand. I didn't see him get up from the table, he's just there. His hair's thick and wavy, a light creamy brown. His eyes are the same shade of green as the sea oats. He smiles as though he's been expecting me and I shiver with recognition. I *know* this guy, but I don't know him. Suddenly, I'm shy. Speechless. Awestruck. And then I wake up.

Dang!

I flip around on my bed so I can get a full view of the framed picture. What's up with this photograph? Two nights in a row. And the guy? I'm sure he isn't someone I've seen before. I hear the Skype ringtone coming from my laptop and it can only be Perry. But I can't talk to him just then. As dumb as it sounds, I feel guilty, like I was dreaming about a real guy and cheating on Perry. Or maybe I was cheating on the dream guy if I talk to Perry at that moment. And I can still feel the sensation I had when I looked into Dream Boy's eyes. Powerful. Intimate. Something I definitely don't want to let go of too soon. And another thing. The headache again. The one that had been slightly nagging the last time. This time it feels like someone's behind my eyeballs, pushing from the inside out.

Aaagh!

FIXING THE AC & MEETING A NEW PERSON . . .

Even though my air conditioner's running at a low roar, I can hear the commotion right outside my window. I get up but Mom isn't around so I go outside to investigate. I find her in the back with Dee, the AC repairwoman. The two of them are hunched over the AC unit, a worker's box of tools by Dee's feet.

"Babe, I'd like you to meet Mrs. Cummings," Mom says. "She's just finished up and we're going inside now to make sure everything works." Then Mom gives me a once-over with her x-ray eyes. "You feelin' alright?"

"Yeah, just a little headache but it's already going away."

"Call me Dee," Mrs. Cummings says. "I'm not a Mrs. anymore, anyhow." She has a really nice smile, the kind that instantly puts you at ease. She has laughing eyes with long, thick lashes. She's pretty for a woman that age—Mom's age. Even when I saw her on the street I could tell.

"You stopped to offer me a ride the other day," I remind her. "I was the one on the bike looking for the Piggly Wiggly."

Dee chuckles. "I was a little worried," she says in a rich drawl. "So how are y'all liking it here so far?"

"I haven't left the house yet," Mom admits. "But Babe . . . she's the adventuress. She's already been exploring." Mom always turns the focus back on me, like she's the PR person in charge of promoting me. It's usually a nice thing until it's not.

"I like it a lot," I say. It isn't really the truth. I actually don't like this town very much, but I don't want to insult Dee Cummings. I'm still hoping Sugar Dunes will grow on me. And I'm still dreading another brand new school where I don't know anyone. "I'm looking forward to starting work next week," I continue to lie in that way proven to please grown-ups.

"Where are you working?" We're inside and Dee's messing with the wall thermostat. A low hum, a pause, and then the air conditioner comes to life.

"The Crystal Point tennis shop." I feel a cool breeze coming from the wall vent above me.

"Really?" Dee turns to look at me. "You might be seeing my son there this summer. He's signed up for a tennis camp some of the young people put together."

"I'll watch out for him. What's his name?"

"Alonso. Actually, *I* signed him up for the camp. Wasn't anything he would've done on his own. He'd rather spend the summer in front of his computer. He's not much for sports but he's a real smart boy. I thought it'd be good for him to get out of the house and get some exercise and, you know . . . mingle with young folk."

Why do adults always think we should mingle with each other? Yeah, sometimes we want to but sometimes we can't stand each other.

I want to say something supportive but I'm skeptical

of parents making kids do things they don't really want to do. Especially tennis, which is one of my favorite things in the world. I hate to see someone being pushed into it against their will.

"If there's anything I can do to help out, just let me know."

I feel this is a pretty safe statement because I doubt there's much I can do to help out but it still sounds good to say it. Mom beams at me.

"Thanks! Like I said, he's a real smart boy. He can practically take apart an air conditioner and put it back together blindfolded. Cars too. I haven't needed a mechanic since he was eleven. But it's just the two of us and he needs to get out some. He'll be starting high school this fall."

Okay, so I met someone new and she's nice and promotes her kid the same way Mom promotes me. I'll probably meet him at some point.

Alonso.

Comments:
Sweetness: okay no offense but i'm more interested in what happened to perry. did i tell you i think i know someone who knows him? anyway, dee sounds cool and i'm all for women doing jobs that usually dudes do but please write more about you and perry. and i don't care that much about dreams because i don't really believe they mean anything.

Babe: I appreciate that you follow my blog but I'm going to write about what interests me so if you don't like it then you don't have to read it. Sorry if that sounds mean but I can't just be taking directions from my readers, you know? I wouldn't tell you what to write on your blog. But thanks for reading anyway and I hope you still keep reading.

Sandman: Hey Baby! Hey Sweetness! How you 2 beautiful ladies doing today?

RoadWarrior: Hello there. I came across your blog while doing research for an upcoming trip my husband and I are planning to the Gulf Coast. I must say it's not the travel blog I expected to find but I'm hooked on your story and love your descriptions. Please keep going. We're retired and hope to be taking our RV down there come November. Best of luck to you.

Babe: Thanks for the follow Road!

DreamMe: Great topic. Hope we get to see more of your Dream Boy.

Babe: Hi DM. Can't say if we will or won't since I write about what's really happening in my life. Thanks for the follow.

ZAT

His last memory is of a pain so deep it can't be endured. And then this. This lightness. He can't get over the lightness and the incredible new strength in his legs. He moves with ease. He picks up objects effortlessly. The pain is gone and Sahra is nowhere to be seen.

Am I dead? Is this what it feels like to die?

He's somewhere white and very bright. He knows bright from the sun that's murdering his Earth, but this isn't that kind of bright. This is a gentle brightness. He looks down at his arms, his legs, his lean but muscular torso covered by a soft, thin material, and he doesn't recognize himself. And yet it's him, he knows that. How do you know when you are you? One only knows and it can't be explained.

He brings a hand to his forehead and then sweeps it

back across the top of his head. Hair. Such an odd sensation but strangely pleasant. A soft rumble plays in his ears. He can barely make it out but it comes and goes in regular intervals. He stands on his now strong legs and looks in the direction of the sound. Beyond the white hills, something sparkles in the distance like a glittering blue jewel.

He must be dead. Only death can bring such lightness. Such freedom.

A chair appears. An umbrella above him casts a shadow over his face. He sits down by the table that has materialized near the chair. Not knowing what to do with his hands, he rests them atop his knees. And he continues to stare in the direction of the rumbling blueness that shines like a gem.

He directs his gaze upwards and is confused by the blueness above him, when he thought it was off in the distance. But the blueness above him is flat. A matte blue unlike the dazzling peek of blue between the soft, white hills.

He stands and then sits. Stands again and then sits again. There's something beyond those white hills. Someone.

Sahra?

He follows the soft rumbling sound to the place where the white hills dip to offer up a glimpse of the glistening blue. He sees her. The girl. Babe.

She's beneath him in elevation. He stands above her by a good two or three body lengths. She's struggling to climb. To him? Can she see him? Does she even know he's there? His heart pounds within his muscled chest walls. It pounds in time with the soft rumble and thump of the blue which he now knows must be the sea. The sea that he's dreamed of since . . . since before he has a memory of not having dreamed of it.

And there's Babe. Climbing. The powerful muscles of her legs straining to deliver her to him. He reaches down, holding his hand out for her, and she looks up at him as though she knows him. As though she has always known him the same way he's always known her.

And then he knows he's arrived.

BABE'S BLOG

GOODBYE PAST . . . HELLO FUTURE!

I find huge dead cockroaches in random places around the house, probably the result of Billy's visit. It's as though what they fear most is dying alone, so they make a mad dash to any well-traveled path where at least their bodies will be discovered. One night at twilight a truck drives slowly down my little street, a fog of insecticide floating in its wake. I hold my breath and run back into the house.

Life here feels wild and dangerous. Only the constant vigilance of Billy the Bug Man and the poison-spewing truck defends us from insect invasion. And the sudden, violent afternoon thunderstorms are a reminder that Mother Nature's in charge and I'd better not forget it.

On Thursday, the moving van arrives and Mom and I transform our house into a home—home being the place where all your junk is. Seeing my possessions again gives me a feeling of continuity. Even though I've just been transported into another world, here come all the things to remind me I'm still me. My book collection, a few stuffed animals I've had since forever, posters, the rest of my clothes and some miscellaneous items I've kept mostly out of habit and loyalty. Being reunited with those otherwise meaningless objects fills me with unexpected joy.

Ever since the night I'd dreamt about the boy who pulled me up the slippery slope of the sand dune, I haven't slept well. Each morning I'm more exhausted than the day before, and my mind feels like mush. Mom is worried I might be coming down with something but I think it's just getting used to my new surroundings. But that isn't me. I've always been able to sleep anytime, anywhere.

By Thursday night, I'm so tired that I'm ready for bed right after dinner even though it's still light outside, but I know Perry will be waiting patiently for my Skype so I go in my room and shut the door behind me. When did this feeling of missing Perry turn into a dreaded feeling of duty? It kills me to feel that way about someone who's made me so happy and been such a supportive friend. I know a lot of my feelings toward him have more to do with security and gratitude but that doesn't make it easier.

"What's up, Babe?" he wants to know after about ten minutes. "You're somewhere else tonight."

"Just tired I guess. Haven't been able to sleep . . . the heat, you know. And everything else."

"I feel like I'm losing you." He looks into the camera

at just the right angle so it feels like he can see inside my head and read my thoughts. I turn away and pretend to search for something inside a desk drawer. This is unexpected. Or is it?

"You're not losing me." How did lying come so easy to me? I hate myself even while I'm saying it. And then a few awkward minutes when neither of us speak. I carry my laptop to the bed and lay down next to it. "Maybe," I begin without knowing where I'm going with this. "Maybe something *is* happening. Maybe we need a few days apart from each other."

"*Apart* from each other? Three thousand miles isn't enough?"

"I meant . . . I meant maybe we should take a break. I don't know what's happening. I can't explain it." Am I such a bad girlfriend our relationship can't survive a week apart from each other? Was I ever really a girl-friend to begin with? Hanging out and doing home-work together and liking the same things doesn't make you a girlfriend, does it? Kissing a little . . . okay, yeah, maybe that says a bit more, but you can still be friends and have some fun can't you? You don't get married to the first guy you make out with. Maybe these are questions I should've thought about before.

"No need to explain." Perry's dark brown eyes look wounded, even a little scared. It frightens me to see him this way. It frightens me to think I have the power to make someone hurt like that. I'd give anything to just fade away but instead he beats me to it and the screen of my computer goes blank.

I don't even bother to get up from my bed. I just close the lid of my laptop and fall into a heavy sleep. Finally, the dream comes.

RETURN OF THE DREAM . . .

I'm walking along the same stretch of beach where I'd seen the café in the past. This time I don't look between the dunes, although the thought of a cold drink and the shade of an umbrella is tempting. It's a perfect day and a Frisbee whizzes past my head on its way from one bronze-backed boy to another. Bikinied girls lay face-down on huge, fluffy beach towels, sizzling themselves into fan-tan-stic golden hues. A fat red man sits in a low beach chair staring out at the waves, a can of beer in his right hand. His arms are folded under the massive roll of his belly as though he's tenderly cradling a stomach-baby. A woman who's probably his wife sleeps on a towel beside him. Her face is covered by an open magazine.

Just like that, the sun's shoved aside by a black cloud that grumbles like a giant's empty stomach. The crowded beach is empty. Huge gray waves claw at the shore and I think I hear someone screaming but it's only the wind.

Before I even see him, I know he's right behind me. I

turn around quickly to bring us face to face.

"I'm sorry," he says. He glows, but not from the sun. "I'm sorry," he repeats miserably.

"I know you," I say. "You're . . ."

"I'm Zat," he says softly. "It's difficult for you. This is . . . difficult for you. I'm sorry for the intrusion."

"Yes," I agree without knowing why.

"I'm the cause of all your pain," he says.

"And all my happiness," I add while feeling totally the opposite of happy, and wondering why those words are coming out of my mouth.

I wake from the dream with a throbbing ache in my forehead that sends me running to the bathroom for aspirin. I've heard of recurring dreams but they're usually the *my-final-exam-is-tomorrow-and-I-missed-every-class* sort. Or even worse, the *my-period-started-unexpectedly-at-school-and-there's-a-bloodstain-on-my-pants* version. But this one was different. Real? Yes, it felt more real than a dream and yet it was a dream. Emotionally intense? All dreams are emotionally intense to some degree. I guess what bothers me is that it seems to be evolving. It's leading me someplace I'm not sure I want to go. And yet the boy, Zat. His mystique is so seductive. I'm pretty sure I'll follow him wherever he wants to go.

Am I trading a real boyfriend for a phantom?

Comments:

Sweetness: yes, i think so.
Sandman: weird
DreamMe: Perhaps you'll have to wait and see where this goes.

Five

My last free day before work and I was deeply in the mood for shrimp. With nothing but wilted vegetables in our refrigerator, seafood became my new passion. I was now officially a pescatarian, and memories of tasty shrimp cocktails weren't all that far in my past.

Nguyen's was packed again, but as soon as I walked in I saw the girl who helped me the last time. She was scooping shaved ice into the display case and using the back of the scooper to smooth the ice into attractive frames for the merchandise. She looked up and grinned.

With a toss of her hair she tilted her head toward the end of the counter where presumably I was supposed to follow her. A long line at the cash register snaked out the door.

"I can help you," she said quietly when we were out of

earshot of the rest of the customers.

Guiltily, I looked over at the long line and noticed a large sweaty man glaring at me.

"Um . . . that's okay. I think I'd better get in line."

"It's okay," she said. "Everyone will think you're a friend of mine. Just laugh and talk like we know each other from school."

"I'm new here, so we couldn't possibly know each other from school."

"They don't know that."

"Why are you pulling me out of line?"

"Look around . . . nobody my age ever comes in here. It's pretty boring."

I looked around and got her point.

"If you're sure it's okay. I'd like a pound of the fresh shrimp."

"All our shrimp is fresh." I winced inwardly at my unintentional insult.

"Are those your parents?" I looked toward the man behind the counter and the woman at the register.

"Yup." She grabbed a few gloves full of shrimp from the bin and wrapped them expertly in butcher paper without even bothering to weigh the package. "I'm pretty good at estimating," she said. "No reason to call attention to ourselves. It should be almost exactly a pound."

The girl's mother spoke loudly across the room in a language I assumed was Vietnamese, and the girl answered in the same language without turning her head.

"Everything okay?" I didn't want her to get in trouble on my account.

"No problem. Do you have six dollars in cash? Just

give it to me." She handed me the packet of shrimp and I dropped it into my backpack, feeling like I was in the middle of an illegal drug transaction.

"Yeah . . ." I fumbled around in my backpack until I located a five and a one. I glanced over at the line of customers again to make sure no one was looking before I paid her. "Where do you go to school?"

"Sugar Dunes High," she said. "It's the only high school in the area. If you live here, you'll go there too."

"What's your name?"

"Mai. Yours?"

"Babe. What grade are you, Mai?"

"I'm going to be a senior finally! Can't wait to graduate and get out of here."

"Me too. I mean, I'm going to be a senior too. Is it really that bad here?"

"Maybe any place where you spend your whole life gets old," she said. "Hey, wanna hang out sometime?"

"That'd be great. Sometime when we're both not working." It was interesting how different our outlooks on life were. I'd have done triple backflips if it bought me more than a year or two in the same school, and Mai couldn't wait to leave.

We exchanged cell phone numbers and then Mai's mom was speaking loudly to her again.

"I gotta give my mom a break at the register. Talk to you later," she said.

Score! I had my first friend.

The next morning Mom and I drove to work with my

dad. Mom was starting her first day in the golf shop, and I was starting in the tennis shop. We were both a little nervous, even though this was nothing new to us. The first week was always the hardest, figuring out how to fit in. We made plans to meet at the hamburger shack by the pool for lunch.

Earl was there when we drove up to the gate, and he greeted us like we were the Royal Family, making all kinds of fuss over us. I must admit, it did help to put me at ease.

"You'll like Bing, great guy," he assured me. Bing was the tennis pro, so I'd be reporting to him. To Mom he said, "You already know how to handle *your* boss, don' choo?"

"I think I have him pretty well figured out," Mom laughed, looking over at my dad.

"Sech a nice-lookin' family. Tell you what, one of these days I'll do a family portrait for y'all down at the beach. Hobby of mine."

"We'll take you up on that, Earl," Dad said.

We drove through the gates to start our new lives at the Crystal Point Resort. *How long will this last?* I couldn't help but wonder.

As it turned out, Bing *was* a nice guy. And a really good looking guy too, although much too old for me. I figured he was probably around thirty, a lot younger than my dad. But playing tennis requires more stamina than playing golf, so it helps to be on the younger side if you're a tennis pro, especially in that heat.

Bing was tall, tan, dark-haired, and definitely not Southern. All the women who came into the shop, young and old, made a beeline for him with all kinds of invented questions and problems apparently only he could solve. It was funny from my perspective. Mostly, I was ignored by the women unless he directed them over to me to fulfill some kind of function like ringing up a purchase or reserving a court. The men, on the other hand, were more interested in checking me out—the new girl, even though I was only seventeen. Lots of pheromones floating around that place. Maybe it was the humidity.

It was so busy I had to work through lunch, so Mom and Dad went without me. The early afternoon was my first opportunity to talk to Bing with no one else around.

"Really slows down this time of day," he said. "The heat gets a bit overwhelming. But pretty soon the younger crowd starts coming in, kids around your age. Maybe you'll make some new friends."

I doubted that. I'd been working in tennis shops since I was fourteen and the kids who came in usually didn't mingle with the paid help. But I wanted Bing to think I was a positive person.

"Maybe. That would be nice." I nibbled on the granola bar he'd offered me earlier in lieu of lunch.

"It's a little different from California, isn't it?" he chuckled.

"It sure is." But in reality I didn't think it was all that different. A country club is a country club no matter where you are. I washed down the dry granola bar with water.

"My last job was in the Virgin Islands . . . St. Thomas,"

he said. "Beautiful place, but you get island fever after a while."

"What's island fever like?"

"You know . . . you get stir crazy like you want to go somewhere but there's nowhere to go. So I took the job here and, so far, I like it. You'll like it too once you get used to the way things are done."

"How *are* things done? Any tips?"

"Tips?" He looked deep in thought before answering. "Okay, here's some advice from one non-southerner to another. The people down here put a premium on manners so a ma'am or a sir will always sound good and you don't have to memorize a lot of names that way."

"Yes, sir," I smirked.

"Now let me give you another piece of advice. People here are very friendly so when you say ma'am or sir, think of it more as someone's name rather than someone's title."

"Yes, *sir*," I said with special emphasis on the second word.

"You catch on quickly, don't you?" He gave me a wink which would have sunk the hearts of all those women who'd been showing off their tanned, toned legs to him earlier in the day. But I wasn't one of those women, and, luckily, Bing had no intentions toward a high school girl like me. "By the way, do you even know how to play tennis?"

"I do."

"Are you any good?"

"I'm alright."

"Just wondering. Every once in a while, one of the ladies might need someone to warm her up while she's waiting for a game. If I'm busy, maybe you could help out."

Somehow I got the feeling a lady expecting a warm-up from Bing would be pretty disappointed if I were substituted in.

"I could do that."

"Thanks, Babe. Naturally, I'll take care of the guys."

Naturally.

The bell on the door jingled to say someone was coming in and our private time was over. Sure enough, just as Bing said, the younger crowd was arriving. The heat of the afternoon drove away the older players and left the courts open for kids my age whose hierarchy I would soon come to know. I remembered what Mai said about there being only one high school so I realized, with a sinking feeling, these people were my future classmates.

Bing had lessons lined up for most of the afternoon, so I was busy selling snacks, balls, and booking courts and ball machines. Normally there would have been three of us working at any given time, but Kay, a lady who usually worked in the shop, was on leave for a month—family emergency. This meant I had to sink or swim. I was determined to swim.

From two until five there was nobody over the age of eighteen at the tennis club except for Bing. Most of them were nice enough, but they didn't care as much as the adults did about the new girl behind the counter.

A couple of times I heard the name Mattie Lynn—as in, "Has Mattie Lynn come in yet?" or "Did you ask Mattie Lynn . . .?" or "Oh my god, Mattie Lynn's new tennis dress is soooo cute." I got the idea that Mattie Lynn was the queen bee. I wondered who the king bee was, even though technically there's no such thing as a king bee. Alpha dog?

About an hour after the initial rush, Mattie Lynn slinked in like a model on a catwalk. I knew it was her the minute I saw her, and the adoring (or was it anxious?) looks on the faces of the other girls at the snack bar confirmed it.

I'm okay in the self-confidence department, but I'm human and therefore susceptible to a little negative self-worth when a physically dazzling person enters a room. So that was my moment. I knew I had to go with it and get it out of the way.

If Mattie Lynn had a physical imperfection I couldn't see it, and I did look. Although we were probably the same height, she seemed taller, a result undoubtedly of her sucking all the oxygen out of the room. I was athletically built. She was athletically built but also had big boobs in addition to her narrow hips and long, lean legs. In her black Stella McCartney mesh tennis dress (yes, I could name the designer of any tennis outfit) her shoulders looked strong and delicate at the same time. I was pale, she was tanned . . . perfectly. My wild, curly, reddish hair was tied into a ponytail with a scrunchy. Her long, glossy brown hair was sleek, thick, and wavy, French braided on the top, loose and tumbling on the bottom—miraculously resistant to heat and humidity.

Okay, I could attract a boy's attention. Hadn't I just kind of broken up with one? But if Mattie Lynn and I were walking down the street together I knew I'd be invisible. But once I checked off the side-by-side physical attributes comparison list, I put it behind me. Lucky for her that she had incredible genes, but I figured she must have some flaws too, even though I didn't see one at the moment. Don't all the beautiful girls in the movies turn out to be evil? Yeah, that must be it. She was probably despicable.

She glided over to the cash register where I was ringing someone up—truthfully, getting someone's signature on their parents' account—and she smiled oh-so-sweetly at me.

"Where's Bing?" she wanted to know. There was no "Hi, I'm Mattie Lynn, welcome to Crystal Point and, by the way, who are you?" Just, "Where's Bing?" Okay, good guess—I knew she wasn't perfectly nice.

"He's on court 5 giving a lesson right now. He should be done in about ten minutes. Can I help you with something?"

Without losing the smile on her face or the honey-dipped southern accent she said, "Are you the new girl?"

Good observation. Who else would I be?

"I'm Babe," I extended my hand across the counter.

She looked at my hand for a brief second like I was trying to pick her pocket or something, but those southern manners kicked in fast and she reached out and gave me the softest, silkiest, non-handshake I had ever experienced. In fact, I wasn't sure when it started and when it was over so I just withdrew my hand after an appropriate length of time. It occurred to me that maybe women didn't shake hands in this part of the world.

Note to self . . . ask Bing about that.

"Mattie Lynn," she said. She probably wasn't used to people not knowing her. "Did Bing talk to you about FAB—the Friends Across the Bay program?"

Bing had mentioned something about it to me. This was the same program Dee spoke of—the one where kids who lived "across the bay" got to spend a few hours a day learning how to play tennis at Crystal Point Resort. *Across the bay*, I quickly learned, was code for the real world inhabited by real people who didn't live in Crystal Point.

"He did say something about it, but we didn't have a chance to discuss it in detail."

Mattie Lynn's smile turned troubled, but still she maintained it.

"I just want to make sure everything's ready," she said. "It starts tomorrow and I want everything to go smoothly the first day."

I wasn't sure why she took this responsibility on her perfectly proportioned and tanned shoulders.

"I'll stay after work and get with Bing on it." I tried to sound reassuring. "He can get me up to speed so I'll be ready tomorrow."

Mattie Lynn's smile turned beautiful again. "Thank yew soooo much," she dripped. "It's sooo important to me."

I admit to being a little impressed it was so important to her. Maybe she actually had a heart. After all, it wasn't her fault she was so beautiful.

"Has LeGrand come in today?" My antennae went up. Could LeGrand be the alpha dog?

"Umm . . . I haven't heard of anyone named LeGrand today."

"If he comes in, please let him know I'm out on Court 3."

"Okay."

"And sooo nice to meet you, Babe. Welcome to Crystal Point. I hope you'll like it here."

I took it. It was the first true welcome I got from a club member the entire day.

LeGrand never showed up, so eventually Mattie Lynn and her entourage got tired of waiting for him and left. I heard one of them say something about how LeGrand wouldn't be arriving until the next day and that made me even more curious—arriving from where? As she was leaving, Mattie Lynn managed a sideways glance in my direction combined with a friendly little wave and a red carpet smile. None of the other girls even looked at me.

My first day on the job kept me busy enough to avoid extreme boredom, but mentally I was checked out by late afternoon, and my mind kept drifting. Every once in a while I had to give myself a virtual slap on the face to return my focus to the task (or person) in front of me. I was beginning to understand why siestas are so popular in hot countries. It's hard to function without one, and I was dragging by the end of the day.

I could have thought about a million different things that day—my job, my life, the sad way Perry looked at me before the computer screen went blank. But I kept coming back to Dream Boy—Zat. How strange I couldn't shake his memory. I had an overwhelming urge to touch him, but he wasn't even real. I remembered the exact sensation I had when he held my hand and helped me up the sliding sand dune. Like being on a first date and already hoping for a second. And third. And fourth and fifth.

"So, you think you could take care of it?" my boss was asking me.

We were alone again, and he'd just locked the door. Closing time.

"Um," I hadn't heard a word Bing said. "Sorry, I have something in my eye. Could you repeat that?"

"Could you call the main club and get sandwiches delivered here around lunchtime tomorrow?"

"Oh yeah, sure. I'll take care of it." Bing was talking about the Friends Across the Bay program, which started the next day. He was anxious for everything to go as planned, so the Queen Bee, Mattie Lynn, would be happy. Or rather, so her parents would be happy, which could only happen if Mattie Lynn was happy.

"You did great today, Babe. Thanks for your help."

"Oh, no problem. Thanks for the job!" I was getting ready to meet my parents and had my hand on the door-knob to leave, but couldn't resist one last question. "Bing, who's LeGrand? I heard a couple of kids talking about him today."

"LeGrand Buell. His parents are big shots around here," Bing chuckled. "They bring their boat to Crystal Point around this time every year and usually spend the whole summer. They're from Memphis. You'll meet them tomorrow because their boat pulled into the marina this afternoon."

"Big shots? I thought everyone here was a big shot."

"True. But Mr. Buell is the king of the hill."

Well at least LeGrand was from Tennessee so he was one less future classmate I'd have to worry about.

"They get the VIP treatment," Bing said. "Of course everyone does, but they get the extra special VIP treatment. They're major investors in the club." Bing raised his eyebrows to make sure I got it.

I already knew everything there was to know about the VIP treatment, extra special and otherwise.

BABE'S BLOG

Walking to the truck after work, Mom and I trade first-day-at-work stories but we're both pretty tired so the conversation fizzles after a few minutes. Dad's happy to have his *girls* by his side so he hardly speaks, but the smile on his face says it all.

I roll down the window during the drive home. After being stuck inside an air conditioned building all day, the heat is a release. It loosens the tight muscles in the back of my neck and shoulders and eases away my tension. It's that special peaceful time just before sunset, when day and night reach equilibrium and the world stops to exhale. I'm never up early enough to know if the world inhales before sunrise.

About a quarter-mile before the Trout Lane turnoff we notice a roadside stand, if you could call it that. Really, it's a sun-faded umbrella that barely throws off enough shade to cover two folding chairs. Seated in one chair is a skinny old man and in the other chair is a plump old lady. In between them, a fat steaming barrel with the torn side of a cardboard box duct-taped to its side. *Boiled Peanuts $1.50* is scrawled in permanent marker on the makeshift sign.

My dad pulls the car off the side of the road.

"You haven't lived until you've tried boiled peanuts," he says.

The old woman doesn't seem excited at the prospect of making a sale. She continues to stare straight ahead at the road, her hands folded across her lap as though daring us to make her stand up. Her gray head is covered with cushiony pink rollers held in place with a scarf tied into a knot at the front of her head. She nods at my dad and me as we approach.

The man is her opposite. All excited by our presence, he flashes a smile that shows so many missing teeth it's hard to envision how he eats. He springs from his chair and walks over to greet us, his head bobbing enthusiastically at the end of a neck that looks too scrawny to support any weight at all. He wears a tank-style undershirt and a pair of baggy denim overalls. He turns his head to the side and hocks a gob of something dark and nasty onto the ground by his feet. It simmers in the sun for a second before vanishing into the sandy soil, leaving only a drab stain to mark the spot where it had been.

"Care for some boiled peanuts today, folks?" Only it sounds like he's saying *biled*.

Dad orders two portions, which the old guy scoops out of the steaming brown liquid I hope is nothing more than peanut-shell-stained water. He wraps them in a newspaper and hands them to me while

Dad pays.

"I don't understand why someone would ruin a perfectly good peanut," Mom says once we're back in the truck. "After all these years, hasn't mankind already perfected the way to prepare it?"

"Don't knock it 'til you try it," Dad says.

And he's right. They're soft and salty and delicious.

I'm exhausted by the time we get home. A bellyful of boiled peanuts has robbed me of my desire for dinner, in fact my stomach is in spasm. I think about calling Perry. I miss him and really need someone to talk to. I wonder how long before we can resume our relationship, forgetting about the love part and carrying on with the friend part. We get each other in a way that's too real to throw away, but I know it's not fair. Do I honestly think I could share my Zat infatuation with Perry? A make-believe boy? I doubt Perry will be ready to transition into friendship any time soon.

When my phone chimes an incoming text, for a second I think it must be Perry. Instead it's Mai, who I never actually expected to hear from outside of the fish market.

Wanna do something tomorrow after work?

And then a few more texts back and forth as to the time, the place, the event. We settle on the Piggly

Wiggly parking lot (where else?) at 6:00 p.m. From there we'll drive together and get dinner at the beach.

I never make it out of my room to say good night to my parents. I just collapse on my bed with the noisy AC wall unit carrying me off into dreamland.

ARE YOU READY FOR THE DREAM AGAIN? I WASN'T . . .

The dream is back.

I'm a little kid riding my bike around Grandpa's neighborhood. This is the only real neighborhood I've ever known outside a country club. Small, but carefully maintained stucco houses line the street. Many of them have red tiled roofs, tidy lawns and walkways that lead straight from the sidewalk to the front doors. Grandpa sits on the front step of his house and watches me turn the corner at the end of the block until I'm out of sight.

"Babe!" I hear him call out. "Babe! Stay where I can see you."

But I can't see him anymore, and I don't know how to get back to the little white stucco house. One house looks exactly like the other. I ride through unfamiliar streets, growing bigger and bigger like Alice in Wonderland until my knees are sore from hitting up against the handlebars. I get off the bike, which is now ridiculously small, and I wonder how I've come so far on a tricycle.

"Were you looking for me?" Zat steps out from behind a leafy maple tree. He smells like cocoa butter. No, he smells like the lavender conditioner I use in my hair. His eyes are one hundred percent pupil, deep and black like a bottomless pit. It feels like I could fall into them, which scares me a little.

"How will I know where to find you the next time?" I ask him.

"I'll always be right here." He reaches out and places the palm of his hand lightly against the contour of my cheek. My face flushes hot at his touch.

"There's so much I want to say to you before you go." I need more time with him. More answers. But he's like sand—slipping through my fingers.

"Say it, then. Please. I *want* to know." Pain over-whelmed me, and I couldn't help but groan, "My . . . stomach . . . hurts . . . so . . . bad . . ."

"I know, Babe."

"You know my name." It isn't a question.

"As you know mine."

"My stomach hurts, Zat. Please don't go."

Then I'm awake, doubled over and perspiring from the pain in my gut. The mob of boiled peanuts is rioting in my stomach which confirms to me there is such a thing as too much of a good thing. My light's still on. I glance at the clock, and it's 3:30 in the morning. I'm still wearing my tennis work outfit.

I go to the bathroom and bend over the toilet, hoping for an end to my misery. No luck with that. Then I sit down on the toilet. A little luck with that. I wander out into the kitchen and gulp down a bottle of water. I go back to bed, undress, and turn off the lights. For the rest of the night I toss and turn, trying to get back to Zat. He told me where to find him but what did he mean? He cradled my face in his hand when he said it.

I want to get back to him and the feeling he stirs up in me.

Except the stomach-pain part.

And of course, the now familiar forehead-hurting part.

Comments:

Sweetness: heres what i think just happened. i think your subconscious is trying to punish you for breaking up with perry. ur headaches are stress headaches becaue you feel so bad for hurting him.

>**Babe:** I wish I knew what my subconscious was trying to tell me. Right now I think it's trying to kill me.

RoadWarrior: Oh my! I have made a note not to try boiled peanuts when we're down there.

DreamMe: He told you everything you need to know.

ZAT

Everything is new, and therefore everything involves a learning curve. The process hasn't been easy. Often it feels like frustration is his dominant emotion.

Learning to weave himself into her dreams is like navigating a maze. His dependence on her is something entirely new and a little frightening. Logic dictates that he must be dependent on Babe, but his dependence goes beyond the parameters of his new world. He feels an emotional dependence quite foreign to him.

Zat has always been a dreamer. A loner. Self-reliant. His family sensed this in him at the earliest age when he set himself apart, establishing himself as separate and unique. When he made the decision to part ways with them, no one was surprised. Everyone knew Zat would create a path uniquely his. His family never doubted the day would come when they'd say goodbye to this beloved and baffling son.

Zat, the dreamer.

Zat, the wanderer.

Zat, the one whom they called Love.

And now the wanderer ends his wandering to wait for the girl who comes to him eagerly, yet sporadically and unreliably.

He must always be prepared. Always vigilant. Always a step ahead in order to find her. If not, he must learn to wait for her to come to him.

This is the balance.

And this is the hardest part.

SIX

I made a point of walking along the marina before work the next morning. I wanted to see the Buells' yacht and how it measured up to the others, considering it belonged to an extra special VIP and all. So I wasn't surprised when I saw *The Lucky Lady*. There wasn't any sign that proved it belonged to the Buells but I had a few clues. First, it was new in the marina, or at least it hadn't been there the last time I walked by. Second, it looked like a baby cruise ship before it grows up. It hogged more than one marina slip and seemed to have its own ecosystem, not to mention a labor pool that was probably bigger than all the other crews combined. It almost blocked out the sun from where I stood.

When I was done gawking, I hurried off to work so I could get there before opening and coordinate the FAB luncheon with the club's kitchen staff. Bing unlocked the door for me and reminded me about ordering the sandwiches the minute I walked in, which was exactly what I was hoping to avoid. I'd envisioned myself greeting him and then going to the phone and calling the kitchen, proving I was able to take charge of a task without being told. I hate having to be reminded of something I'm just about to do. If Bing was my dad I would've said, "I know. I was just gonna do it." But of course I couldn't talk back to Bing like that, so I just smiled and picked up the phone.

I began to fixate on the Buells as a way to alleviate my boredom at work. If they had everyone else buzzing with excitement then they should be entertaining, or at least distracting. Mattie Lynn and LeGrand were *the* story—it didn't take me long to catch on.

I didn't have to wait long for them to show up. Only an hour after opening, Mr. and Mrs. Buell made their grand entrance. I immediately noticed the change in Bing when Mrs. Buell offered him a lazy hand in greeting.

"So good to see yew, Bing," she drawled.

Her platinum blond hair was perfectly done in a French twist updo. Either she was a hair styling genius or they had a stylist on staff at *The Lucky Lady*. And Mrs. Buell for sure was one lucky lady. They say people "drip" diamonds. Well, she had a total downpour going on. A huge rock weighed down her left hand, a platinum string of diamonds encircled her right wrist, and her earlobes weren't spared. She was beautiful, of course. Could she be Mrs. Buell and not be beautiful? But her face was tightly pulled back, which always makes me cringe. Still, it was fun to observe her, in a reality show kind of way.

Mr. Buell was tall, silver-haired, and elegant, which made me wonder why men could be silver-haired and still considered handsome, but if women were silver-haired they were considered old. He looked like he should be drinking a mint julep or at least something like it. Not that I knew what a mint julep was, but it sounded like something you would drink if you were rich and living in the South.

Note to self: taste a mint julep.

I was ready to give the Buells the extra special VIP treatment which would have been the same treatment I gave everyone else, when I caught Mr. Buell giving me the eye. That is, *the eye* in a flirtatious sense. He looked me up and down and then went back to his conversation with his wife and Bing. Could he really be looking at me that way? Seventeen-year-old me? With his wife standing mere inches away?

After some more chatting about upcoming singles tournaments, and getting some help from Bing with his serve and his wife's tennis elbow, the Buells decided they'd better get out on the court before it got too hot. They were going to hit with each other that day, since they had a luncheon planned for some friends on the boat, and Mrs. Buell wanted to get back to supervise preparations.

At one point Bing mentioned my name and pointed in my direction. I put on my friendliest, most helpful smile, and Mrs. Buell swiveled her frozen face in my direction and returned my smile with what I would describe as a semi-friendly gaze. Mr. Buell looked over at me and nodded all business-like. Then he followed his wife out the door, racket in hand. When he shifted his body to close the door behind him—which wasn't necessary because it was the kind of door which closed by itself—he looked at me again. That time there was no mistaking the look he gave me. It sent shivers through my body. The bad kind.

The rest of the morning was much like the day before. I was busy inside while Bing was busy outside. I honestly don't know what he would have done without me there since Kay was on leave. I suppose they would have sent someone over from the golf shop to help out—they had more funding and therefore a bigger staff. But I liked to think I was making myself indispensable since I already knew so much about the tennis scene and didn't require much instruction.

After lunch the Club sent over the sandwiches, cookies, and lemonade I ordered for the Friends Across the Bay program, which was supposed to start at two o'clock. Already some of the participants were straggling in, wanting to get there early for the first day. I could spot them from their anxious expressions. A few of them knew each other and sat quietly in a corner, occasionally whispering, but mainly just looking around pretending to be disinterested. I wondered how many of them were there against their wills, forced by their parents, like Alonso, to do something out of their comfort zones. I also wondered how many of them would view this experience as a positive event in their lives after a month under Mattie Lynn's supervision.

The adults cleared out and the young club members trickled in. I counted twelve kids who I was pretty sure were FAB participants. Twelve was the magic number so I went over and directed them to help themselves to the refreshments—thin, crustless white bread sandwiches and huge, chunky gourmet cookies. This inspired only a little bit of interest, probably because most of them had likely already eaten lunch before arriving.

Half of the group was African-American, in stark contrast to the mentors, who were all white. The other half was white, with the exception of one Asian boy, who looked very small, very young, and very shy. I'd have to keep an eye out for him if he didn't partner up with someone I considered nurturing enough. I could already tell he had the potential to break my heart.

Of the African-American kids, I tried to guess which one was Alonso, and I came to a quick conclusion. Three of them were boys, and two of them looked fairly athletic. Only one looked like the type of kid whose muscles were underdeveloped—probably the result of TMCT, an acronym my dad invented when we were younger for Too Much Computer Time. TMCT was considered a bad thing by my parents. The three boys stood off to the side, separated from the others.

Since I promised Dee I'd check up on Alonso, I walked over to the boy I assumed was him. "Are you Alonso?" I asked.

He shook his head, "No, I'm James." So much for my powers of observation.

I looked over at the other two boys who were standing within earshot. One of them immediately looked down at the ground. The other one smiled at me and nudged the one looking at the ground.

"He's Alonso," the smiling boy finally said when there was no response from the nudged, ground-looking boy.

Alonso had his mother's beautiful skin and warm looks.

"I'm Babe," I said to the three of them. James suppressed a giggle which was, I suppose, the result of hearing my name. "Alonso, I know your mom," I went on.

"I know. She told me." He looked everywhere but at me—the wall, the floor, James, the cookies . . . everywhere.

"I just wanted to introduce myself and let you know if you need anything, any of you, please don't hesitate to ask me."

"Thank you, ma'am," James said. Ma'am? Did I look that old? I was probably only two or three years older than these guys.

"Thanks," the smiling boy said as he nudged Alonso again.

"Yeah, thanks," Alonso said to the sandwiches.

"Can I have everyone's attention please," Mattie Lynn rapped the side of a glass with a metal spoon. I wondered where she picked up that move. "I think we're all here now and I'd like to welcome our friends from across the bay." She seemed genuinely happy. The others applauded enthusiastically as though Mattie Lynn had just announced the nominees for Miss Teen USA.

"I'll be calling out your names so please listen to hear who you'll be partnered with. Mentors, please introduce yourself to your friend when you hear your name called."

Bing was watching from the sidelines. He looked

on approvingly but nervously, ready to get involved if anything went wrong but relaxed enough to know he probably wouldn't be needed. After all, this was supposed to be a "youth-directed" community outreach program.

Mattie Lynn went down the list saying things like, "Leanne, please welcome Emma. Emma is fourteen and likes to dance. Her favorite color is red." I swear Mattie Lynn was a natural for something, I'm just not sure what that something was.

The little Asian kid who stole my heart was one of the last to be called. He was already wringing his hands when Mattie Lynn finally called his name.

"Kiet is twelve and is a fan of NASCAR. His favorite color is blue, and he hopes to be an astronaut when he grows up." All the girls cooed over him like a flock of pigeons.

"He's super cute," I heard one member of Mattie Lynn's posse whisper to another, as if they were twenty years older than him. But I must admit, he was pretty adorable.

"Kiet will be with me," Mattie Lynn announced proudly. I wasn't sure if I was horrified or thrilled for him. He would be well cared for under her protective umbrella.

Only Alonso remained and there was an uncomfortable pause in the welcoming ceremony as Mattie Lynn nervously scanned the room. All of a sudden her face lit up and she resumed speaking. I followed her gaze to the doorway, the place where her expression had transformed from worry to delight.

A slender, tallish guy about my age leaned against the wall, his front leg resting at an angle. Arms crossed across his chest and a bemused expression on his face, his dark blond hair was sort of wind-swept and shaggy in a very chic way. He had steely blue eyes with perpetually half-closed lids that said, *I'd rather be somewhere else but you've got my attention for now.* The corners of his lips were barely turned up in a half-smirk like he'd just heard a joke no one else would ever get. There was nothing second rate about him, in physical appearance at least. LeGrand Buell had finally made his appearance.

"And last but not least is Alonso, who loves computers and fixing things. He's fourteen years old, and his favorite food is Italian. Alonso will be paired with LeGrand, who has just joined us."

At that announcement, all the female heads in the room swiveled around every which way looking for the star of the show. Soft murmurs of delight could be heard once their target was spotted. LeGrand ambled up to the place where Alonso stood and performed one of those left hand on the shoulder, right hand in a handshake moves guys pull off so well. LeGrand was talking and Alonso appeared to be listening, even making eye contact every once in a while.

After the welcoming ceremony everyone went out to the courts and I was left alone with Bing for the next few hours. I cleaned up the luncheon table. Barely any of the food had been touched so Bing told me to take home whatever I wanted. I packed away enough sandwiches and cookies for my family's dinner that night, even though I'd be eating out with Mai. No sense in letting expensive club food go to waste.

After a few hours, cars started pulling up in the tennis

club parking lot which I figured must be the parents of Friends Across the Bay participants. I even saw the white pick-up truck with "Cummings Emergency AC Repair" on its side. Some of the kids came through the club on their way to meet parents, helping themselves to the icy cold water bottles I'd laid out on the luncheon table. Others skipped the clubhouse and walked all the way around the building to get to their parents' cars. It was hard to tell what they were thinking after this first day of tennis camp because everyone wore the same exhausted and heat-swamped expression on their faces. I wondered how many of the twelve would be back the next day.

Mattie Lynn and a few of her maidens-in-waiting lingered, talking about their "friends," plotting the next day's strategy, and obviously just waiting to see what LeGrand was going to do next.

LeGrand was floating around, checking out a new tennis racket, sipping from a water bottle. He seemed to be oblivious to the sensation he created around him. He was like a magnet, pulling people toward him, but when they got too close, they bumped up against the force field keeping them at a safe distance. LeGrand had the power of confidence, but more than that, confidence combined with indifference. A deadly combination when it came to adoring female fans. I wasn't completely immune.

As he drifted, he came closer and closer to my work station until, all of a sudden, he was standing right in front of me. Like looking out the window of an airplane, you feel as if you're suspended in air and then an hour later you're 500 miles away. That was LeGrand. Just as you got a fix on him in one place, he was already somewhere else.

"I haven't seen you here before." His drawl was ridiculously sexy.

"That's because this is only my second day of work."

"That so? Where y'all from?"

Mattie Lynn watched from the corner of her eye. I knew that for a fact because I was watching her out of the corner of *my* eye.

"California," I said. No need to go into all those other places I was from. California was the most recent and sounded the coolest.

"That so?" he said again. "I've been to California a few times. I'd like to go again."

"It's a great place." I wasn't very good with small talk.

"Well, I guess I'll see you tomorrow. Bye." Which sounded like "bah" as in "bah bah black sheep."

He moseyed out the door, and Mattie Lynn, noticing his departure from the corner of her other eye, quickly disengaged from the meaningless conversation she was carrying on and ran after him. I saw her through the window as she jogged a few steps to catch up with LeGrand. The two girls she left, mid-sentence, looked foolishly at each other, completely lost without their leader. After a few minutes they left too.

Seven

My cell phone chimed an incoming text.

M: Where are you?
B: In the Piggly Wiggly parking lot. Where are you?
M: In the Piggly Wiggly parking lot too.

I looked around the massive lot but saw no sign of Mai. Before I could ask for her car's description, she texted again.

I'm in the part closest to the street.

I squinted my eyes in the dimming light and, way off in the distance, I saw a little blue car parked all by itself with about a football field of space around it in every direction. She was standing next to it, waving.

Okay I see you. I'll drive over there and park where you are.

When I pulled up next to her, the breeze blew my first paycheck out the window of the truck. I jumped out and followed it onto the grassy strip in front of us, but Mai beat me to it and grabbed the check before it could blow onto the street. Then her hand darted out and she gripped my arm.

"Watch out, you almost stepped on a fire ant nest."

I looked down at my feet and saw the telltale sandy hump, but there wasn't enough light to see the little devils themselves.

"I'll never get used to this," I said plaintively.

"Yes you will. 'Specially if you ever step on one." That was reassuring.

We decided to go to a place Mai recommended right on the beach—Alligator Al's. She said the food was great, and it was casual and fun. Little did I know I would actually be eating alligator at Alligator Al's. I hesitated at first, still remembering the boiled peanuts, but decided to go for it and was glad I did. It was delicious, like a cross between chicken and fish. How had I transformed so quickly from a vegetarian to a gobbler of reptiles? Entering the world of Sugar Dunes was like shedding the skin of everything I was before. In the name of healthy eating, I also ordered a side of okra and black-eyed peas, but I knew the frying-in-lard part negated any benefit.

After dinner we walked along the beach. I figured if we walked for the next twenty hours I might come out even on the calories consumed for dinner. It was still hot out, and there were plenty of people on the beach even though it was almost dark. The sunset was even more amazing than the Mississippi mud pie that Mai and I shared for dessert.

This was the first time I'd actually gone in the ocean since we moved to Sugar Dunes. We kicked off our flip flops and walked along calf deep in the water. It was warm enough that in some parts of the world it might actually be considered suitable hot tub temperature. Not particularly refreshing on a hot summer day, but sublime on a warm summer night.

It turned out Mai and I had a lot in common. Well maybe nothing really in common, but a lot to talk about and conversation came easy.

"I heard about that Friends Across the Bay program." Mai rolled her eyes. "Friends . . . what a joke. More like 'Pad Your College Application' program. I've never seen any of those people on *my* side of the bay."

"You never know." I was protective of tennis and always held out hope someone might be inspired with the love of the game the way I was.

"So you're one of *those* people who makes life wonderful for Mattie Lynn," Mai said, allowing me instant access to her feelings about Mattie Lynn.

"I guess you could say that. But if I am then I'm also making life wonderful for me too."

"How's that?"

"I need a job, don't I?"

"Okay, I get your point. That Kiet kid, I know him. His mom and my mom are friends. He won't last more than two days. He's a brat."

"A brat?" That didn't fit with the image of an adorable, sensitive boy I'd conjured up. "He seems so sweet."

"Yeah, well looks can be deceiving," Mai said in her

soft lilt. "Trust me, I've known him since he was born. Spoiled rotten by his parents because it took them so long to have a kid."

"Do a lot of . . . Vietnamese people live around here?"

"We have a pretty big community. And you don't have to feel embarrassed to ask, it's not a dirty word or anything," Mai laughed, picking up on my awkwardness.

"Do your mom and dad speak English?"

"My mom not so good, but my dad is fluent. They've been here a long time. Since they were my age. Way before I was born."

"Why *here*? I mean, why's there such a big Vietnamese community in Sugar Dunes?"

"They were fishing people in Vietnam. After the war, the ones who could get out of the country left. A lot of them might've been killed if they were identified with the old regime. Boat people is what they were called back then, which drove my parents crazy . . . like they were somehow less than other people. So my grandparents put my mom on a boat and never saw her again. They weren't even sure if she would survive, but they thought that whatever happened it'd be better for her than living under the Communist government."

"Why didn't they go with her?"

"They didn't have enough money. In our culture, parents do everything to give their kids a chance for a better life."

"Do your parents miss their home?"

"This *is* their home. They're both citizens and my sister and I were born here. I guess in the beginning it was hard. The local fishermen were threatened by the competition from all the new fishermen, so there was violence against the Vietnamese. And, for some strange reason, they blamed the refugees for the war, as if they had anything to do with it. They were innocent victims but Americans didn't want to think about the war anymore and people like my parents were a constant reminder."

"Wow, that sounds—"

"Things have changed a lot. I was born here and I never saw any of that shit happening. I've only heard about it from my parents."

"So why'd you say you can't wait to get away from here?"

"It gets old real fast. There's nothing to do but go to the beach and work and go to school. I'm only applying to colleges in cities with a million or more population: NYU, UCLA, Emory, Tulane . . ."

Warm, silky wavelets lapped against my legs, and I felt the balmy blush of sunset. "Be careful what you wish for," I said. "To some people, this might be paradise."

"Paradise, hah!" Mai scoffed at the notion. "Hey, I know that guy. He comes in the store a lot."

Walking toward us, with a big grin on his face, was Earl. I didn't recognize him at first outside of the gatehouse in his civilian clothes. He was even smaller on the beach with no shoes to add the extra few inches to his height. He was loaded down with some elaborate and expensive looking camera equipment.

"If it isn't two of my favorite gals!" he said.

"It was Earl who told me about your family's market," I said.

"That's right." He looked at Mai. "You can thank me

for your new friend here."

Mai smiled sweetly and immediately went into behind-the-counter customer service mode. "How are you, Mr. Collins?"

"Just call me Earl. Some days I'm not even sure who Mr. Collins is." He chuckled at his joke. "I'm fine, jes' fine. Thought I'd come out and take a few photos of the sunset. Photography's a hobby of mine, you know."

Even if he hadn't already mentioned this multiple times since I'd met him, it would be pretty easy to figure out from the looks of his equipment. "How about a quick pose, you two? There's jes' enough light for a real pretty sunset shot."

This was my second pose for Earl and I wondered what he did with all the pictures he took. But he did get our cable fixed and maybe he'd give me a copy of the picture. Mai and I posed with just the faintest pink sky behind us. Physically, we were an odd contrast in just about every way. It would make for an interesting portrait, I thought.

Afterward, Earl strolled down the beach and Mai and I continued our walk.

"You don't think he's some kind of a pervert, do you?" she asked.

"I don't think so." I didn't think it was too strange of a question, with all the warnings girls our age get from their parents. "I think he just likes taking pictures. At least I hope so, and—"

"—photography's a hobby of his." We both said it at the same time, laughing while we did.

"Do you know how he pronounced your last name?

Nuggins!"

"You think that's funny? How do *you* pronounce it?"

"I'm not saying I know exactly how, but I know it's not Nuggins."

"Go ahead. Take a stab at it."

"Nuh-goo-yen?" I said hesitantly.

"Now *that's* funny, Babe. Honestly." Her laugh came out like a short snort.

I reached over and playfully yanked her pony tail. "Okay, Nuggins. Be careful what you wish for."

BABE'S BLOG

Does it seem strange that I couldn't wait to get home last night and go to sleep so I could dream about Zat? It doesn't seem strange to me. When my family lived in Nevada I had a friend who was bipolar. She sometimes got herself into trouble by skipping her meds. The way she explained it to me was the meds took away that creative rush that came with her highs and she didn't want to give up that part of her life. I think I know how she felt, although I'd never condone someone skipping their meds. My Zat dreams are something I probably should talk to someone about. The headaches are a red flag and I've never heard of a person having sequential dreams. Sometimes I wonder about my own sanity. But the anticipation of spending an evening with him keeps me going during the day. The excitement and rush of emotions make me protective of my dreams, and therefore secretive. If I tell my parents, will he go away? Am I an idiot for sharing it in this blog?

Have any of you out there had an experience like this? Where you fall in lust with someone you meet in your dreams? Where that person feels more real and more interesting than anyone you know in your real life? Where that person keeps coming back again and again, night after night, until you feel you know him as well as you know anyone in your waking world? Maybe even better?

Yesterday I met a guy at the tennis club. He's kind of awesome but I know it's just his looks. The way he talks and carries himself. His style. With Zat, he's awesome for sure. And he's hot too. But he's also attuned to me. My moods. My insecurities. My passions. And I'm attuned to him in the same way. So much that I can sometimes feel what he's going to say before he even says it.

THE DREAM, PART 4 OR 5 OR SOMETHING LIKE THAT (I'VE LOST TRACK) . . .

I run up the stairs of a huge cement building, keeping one hand on an old metal railing that smells like pennies. Each floor has four or five numbered apartments but I know which one I'm looking for so I keep climbing, out of breath, rushing to get there before the door's locked. I see the number on the door, 758. It's open just a crack. A beam of sunlight slices through the opening, a golden wedge that penetrates the gloom of the dark building.

I walk through the doorway and step into the room, which opens into a garden beautifully neglected by human hands. A tangle of pansies, snapdragons, daffodils and poppies grow helter skelter between the cracks of an old cobblestone path. The path, I know, will lead me to Zat if I stay on it. But sometimes, when the overgrowth is too thick, I have to bend down and push the grass aside so I can feel my way forward.

When I finally see him, he's sitting on an old wooden bench. He looks up and smiles.

"You found me quickly this time," he says.

"I knew where to look."

I sit near him on the bench. The empty space between us feels as wide as a canyon. Then, once again the sky turns mean and black, and thunder rumbles in the distance. Cold silver pellets of rain fall from the sky, drenching my clothes and I shiver uncontrollably. Zat puts his arm around me and pulls me close. I lean into him, my cheek resting against his chest. I can hear the steady thump of his heart-beat. The steady pounding of waves. My spine tingles. He grazes the top of my head with his lips and my hair stands on end. His hand slides up my ribs until it's resting lightly on the side of my breast. My breath comes out ragged and my mind's a blissful mess of mush.

And then a thump on my window wakes me. Dang! A bat with faulty sonar? A prowling burglar? I don't care. I only want to get back to sleep. Get back to Zat and whatever it was we were about to do.

Don't move a muscle, Babe, I hear him say in my half-waking state. *Don't get up to pee. Don't open your eyes.*

Then he's swimming beside me in a calm sea. I felt brand new, weightless, suspended in the warm salty water. This must be what it feels like to be in the womb, to be unborn and to only know sounds and sensations. Are we wearing clothes? I'm not sure. He holds my hand and turns me to face him. Our heads bob above the water while coral-colored minnows dart between my legs and brush up against my bare belly.

"Can I touch your hair?" he asks.

"Of course."

He squeezes a handful of my hair which is curiously dry even though we're in the water.

"It's nice," he smiles. "It feels . . ."

"Feels?"

"It feels fat."

"Fat?"

"That's a good thing, right?"

"Fat? My hair is fat?"

"I'm sorry. I can't think of a word equal to your hair. This is the one that seems best. Full. Firm. Fat."

"Okay," I laugh. "I'll take it."

"Are we swimming?"

Until that point I'd forgotten we were in the ocean. I look down and see my legs and his legs, white and wavy beneath the surface. Distorted by the prism of the ocean's surface.

"We're treading water."

"Is that swimming?"

"Sort of. You ask funny questions."

"I'm a nuisance?"

"No, you're just different."

"Is it alright to hold you while we tread water together?" Without waiting for an answer he puts a hand on either side of my waist. We're unbelievably buoyant, rising above the water from the waist up. I have a moment of relief when I realize I'm wearing a bikini top.

I'm a strong person, more athletic than a lot of guys. So it surprises me to feel delicate in his arms. And for the very first time with a guy, I realize I don't have to surrender my power to enjoy his.

"I want to be with you always," I blurt out.

"Why?"

"Now I know what it feels like to belong with someone."

"You might change," he said. "It's still new. Everything's new."

"I'll never change."

"I've known you for a very long time, Babe. Sometimes it seems like I've been thinking about you my whole life. But you know nothing about me."

"Then tell me."

"I'm afraid you won't like what you hear."

"You scare me when you talk like that. Why wouldn't I like what I hear?"

"Why wouldn't I like what I hear?" I repeat when he doesn't answer.

"Why wouldn't I . . ." I'm really talking now. Talking out loud in the real nonsleeping world. It's never been so hard to wake up. Daylight intrudes through the window blinds in golden stripes of light. I fight it with all my might but the drone of the air conditioner and my parents' busy morning footsteps force my eyes open. I drag my legs over the side of the bed.

Sixteen more hours until bedtime, I think. *Sixteen long, miserable hours.*

My head hurts with an intensity which terrifies me.

Comments:

Sweetness: girl im worried about you. youd better go see a doctor or something.
RoadWarrior: I'd have to say I agree with Sweetness. Headaches can be a sign of something serious. Please get it checked out by a doctor.
DreamMe: When the dream becomes too much to contain . . .

Babe: Thanks for your concern everyone. I'll figure it out.

EIGHT

There was a message waiting for me from Mattie Lynn on the tennis club voicemail. *No need for lunch since nobody seemed interested yesterday. Just make sure there are lots of chilled water bottles.* I wondered who would be back after the first day. I especially wondered about Kiet, whom Mai predicted would be an early dropout.

The adult crowd was ready to go first thing in the morning. Bing spent most of his time outside giving lessons to anyone who could afford to hang out at the tennis courts in the middle of a work day. That included his usual following of pampered and adoring housewives, independently wealthy men, and retired people of both sexes. All the working adults came after work and on the weekends.

My place, as usual, was inside answering phones and

generally taking care of whatever needed taking care of. I didn't mind because it was so hot outside, even in the morning, but I did miss actually being able to play tennis. I worried my game would get rusty since I still didn't have a partner, although Bing promised he'd make time for me when things slowed down.

Mrs. Buell came in early to play doubles with some ladies I hadn't seen before. With her perfect hair, she looked so cool that you could never imagine her working up a sweat. She probably bathed in ice water, and even Bing's charms had no effect on her. Style. She had plenty of it, but it was pretty clear we were never going to be buddies.

The Sullivans came in later. I fell for them the first time I met them. They were both in their late seventies to early eighties and probably as fit as their children, if they had any. They rode their bikes everywhere, chatted with me on a real level like they actually cared about me, and when I tried to "sir" or "ma'am" them, they shushed me and insisted I call them Bob and Dotty. Bing said they were involved in all kinds of community service and basically everyone loved them because, after all, what wasn't there to love?

Bing came in for a short break. Mr. Buell had a lesson scheduled but hadn't showed up yet. It actually was billed as a lesson but, according to Bing, Mr. Buell just paid him to play. Lessons were probably beneath him. When I asked how good he was, Bing just said Mr. Buell wasn't nearly as good as he thought he was. After waiting about ten minutes, Bing went back out to the courts to pick up tennis balls.

Soon after, Mr. Buell came in, not even apologizing for being late. He asked where Bing was and I said he was waiting outside. Mr. Buell took his sweet time messing around with this and that. I glanced at the clock and noted that Bing's next lesson would start in ten minutes. How was he going to handle the extra special VIP problem?

Then Mr. Buell did something strange. He leaned across the counter where I was working and started snooping around. He spotted my blog journal which was right next to my purse on the shelf behind the counter. I took it to work to take notes during breaks. On the cover of the journal in bold black marker it clearly said BABE'S BLOG. If I wore it on a chain around my neck it couldn't be more obvious who it belonged to. Normally I kept a huge rubber band around it to keep it protected, but earlier that morning the rubber band had snapped.

Mr. Buell just picked it up like it was a National Geographic in the dentist's office and made a movement to open it. My hand shot out and held the cover down. Our eyes met and locked, mine in a dare that said, *I dare you to open my journal.* His in a dare that said, *I dare you to lose your job.* He put his hand on top of mine, moving his thumb back and forth, all the while maintaining eye contact. Then he pulled his hand away and smiled creepily. He reeked of alcohol.

"Sorry, darlin'. I didn't know that was yours."

Like hell he didn't.

The door opened with a chime of the bells and Bing walked in.

"Mr. Buell, are you ready to go out now?" It seemed

the lesser VIP's lesson would be sacrificed to Buell.

"I don't think so, Bing. Just came by to let you know it didn't work out for me today." He winked at me and turned to leave.

I wanted to kick his ass so bad I could scream.

There was a lull around 11:30, so Bing and I took advantage and had a quick lunch. With no lessons scheduled and no courts booked, we just put up the "Back in ___ minutes" sign and filled in "30" with a dry erase marker. I think Bing could tell something was wrong, even though I tried to hide it and denied it when he brought it up. No way was I going to let Mr. Buell come between me and my job, as much as I'm sure he would have enjoyed a me-against-him scenario. It was nothing more than a game to him, but for me it wrecked my entire day.

Mattie Lynn slinked in early in another Stella McCartney tennis ensemble. I guessed she never wore the same outfit two days in a row, and there I was on day three wearing my inexpensive, low-fashion tennis dress. It was cute, short, functional, and all I could afford. But I realized I'd have to get another one soon or risk sparking a fashion scandal.

Mattie Lynn glanced at the buckets which I'd filled with ice and stocked with bottled water.

"Nice job, Babe," she flashed the results of thousands of dollars of orthodontic work at me. "Are any of our *friends* here?"

"Nobody's come yet."

"I'm just going to warm up for a few minutes with the ball machine. I'll be back in ten. Oh, and if LeGrand comes in early, can you tell him I'm out back please?"

"No problem."

"Thank yew so much. You're such a doll, helping out."

There are compliments which make you feel good, and compliments which make you feel worthless. I'm sure Mattie Lynn meant to deliver the former, but unfortunately it had the impact of the latter.

I sat on the high stool behind the counter and leaned forward, my hands supporting the weight of my head, elbows propped on the counter. My hair made a curtain on either side that, for a few seconds, shut out the rest of the world. I thought about Mr. Buell and the sneering parting look he gave me.

I thought about Zat.

I'm afraid you won't like what you hear, he'd said. And then he left me hanging. Or I'd left myself hanging by waking up. I could still feel the pain. The pressure behind my eyes.

And yet I ached to go back to sleep.

I was surprised to see so many kids arriving early. Kiet was the first, bounding in with an actual smile on his face, wearing very short white shorts and a white polo shirt with a broad red stripe through the center. He was still adorable and you could tell he was pleased as a peacock with the way he looked, probably thinking of himself as handsome and studly as opposed to adorable. The others soon followed and I noticed most of them headed straight to the table where lunch had been set out the day before, and where only ice water waited for them that day.

"Are we too early for lunch?" James asked me.

"Umm . . . there *is* no lunch today." It became apparent the day before they were all post-lunch but that day they'd skipped lunch, expecting sandwiches at the club.

"Oh man," James turned to the smiling boy who I now knew was named LaShawn. "I'm starving. Did you eat?"

"Nope."

They weren't the only hungry ones. Everyone who came in, *friend* and *mentor* alike, made a pass by the table only to turn away in disappointment once they realized there was no food. I guiltily sold some snack bars we carried at the shop to the ones who had money in their pockets. And I sneaked one of my own into Kiet's hands.

Alonso was off standing by himself so I went to check in with him, still feeling my responsibility after that brief conversation with his mom.

"So what did you think about tennis camp yesterday. Did you have fun?"

"It was good," he addressed my feet in a completely unconvincing voice.

I could tell Alonso was the one who least liked being here, but I also had a sense for his mother's determination, so I knew he'd be here every day for the entire month.

Still no LeGrand. He was probably one of those people who lived by a dramatic life script which included a lot of late entrances. Mattie Lynn came in from court-side and the energy that had been scattered around the room coalesced like a puffy white cloud above her head. Kiet maneuvered his way through the bodies to stand possessively next to her.

"Kiet! So good to see you. I hope you rested well last night and are ready for some really hard work today." She put a perfectly tanned arm around his shoulders and gave him a friendly squeeze.

He smiled up at her and nodded. No hand wringing today.

I could see Mattie Lynn taking a mental head count, which I'd already done. Only nine *friends*. All the mentors were present with the exception of LeGrand.

"I suppose we should wait a few minutes for the others to get here," she said. Only the tiny indent between her eyebrows betrayed her anxiety. "Let's go over yesterday's program and address any concerns or problems anyone might have." She was so good.

Finally, Mattie Lynn was forced to accept that the missing friends and LeGrand weren't going to show up. I actually felt sorry for her, and for Alonso, too. I hoped he didn't take it personally, but how could he not? Since there were extra mentors with nothing to do, Alonso was reassigned to a girl named Suellen. The group exited to the courts, traipsing after Mattie Lynn like a flock of ducklings.

I stuck my head out a few times to get a feel for how good the players were, hoping I might find a future hitting partner who would match up with my skills. Suellen and Mattie Lynn had decent ground strokes, although I questioned whether either of them would ever want to play with me.

Alonso's "lesson" consisted of Suellen hitting the ball right to him while yelling in a way-too-loud voice, phrases she probably thought were motivating, like "Go for it, Alonso!" or "Pick up the pace!" or, after a while, "C'mon, you're here to learn aren't you?!"—which he clearly wasn't.

Alonso's passive aggressive response was to move even more slowly, to the point that only when Suellen aimed directly for the face of his racket did a ball ever bounce off of it. Then, with the speed of a snail, he'd trudge over to pick up the wayward ball despite Suellen's protests they wait until the end to do that.

It was painful to watch, and after a while I couldn't take it anymore, so I went back inside.

At some point, about halfway through the program, LeGrand sauntered in looking like he'd just woken up. His hair was even scruffier and his eyes even sleepier than the day before. He veered off to the luncheon table, perhaps looking for coffee and a donut, and finding nothing but water he looked over at me and grinned sheepishly.

"Whoops . . . I guess I missed lunch today."

I was angry at him. I couldn't begin to comprehend the mindset of people like the Buells who live by rules that don't apply to everyone else. He'd made a commitment to Mattie Lynn . . . to Alonso. How much did that mean to him? Apparently nothing.

"There was no lunch today." I tried to keep all the humor out of my voice and it wasn't hard since I was still furious with his father.

"So what part of California are you from?" Lunch

didn't seem to be a big deal.

"I think Alonso's out there . . . if you were planning on working with him today."

"Alonso? He's here? No shit?"

"Well, yeah!" I knew I wasn't delivering the extra special VIP treatment but I was really pissed off.

"He told me yesterday he was dropping out of the program and I asked him to text me last night to let me know for sure. Which he did."

This actually had me a little perplexed. It didn't fit with the whole scenario I'd constructed in my head, the one where LeGrand would be the convenient repository for all my hatred of his father.

"Oh. I guess he must have changed his mind because he's here, hitting with Suellen."

"Hot dog! I'd better go rescue him in that case. Hitting with Suellen will guarantee he won't come back."

By then he was standing right next to me, having pulled off one of those mystifying moves where you don't even realize he's in motion until he's there. Maybe he wasn't like his dad, I'd have to give him the benefit of the doubt. But there was one way they were alike which was obvious at that point. They both smelled of alcohol in the middle of the day.

The ranks of the *friends* dwindled as the days went on until, by the end of the first week, only six seemed likely to stay. Those six, mostly boys, included Kiet, who was blossoming before my eyes; Alonso, who was dying before my eyes; and James and LaShawn, who were both showing a lot of promise in tennis and seemed to enjoy the game.

With every kid who dropped out of the program, Mattie Lynn focused even more intensely on Kiet. At first I thought it was because losing her personal *friend* would have been devastating not only to the program's future but also to her own self-worth. But it became clear she genuinely liked Kiet, and he was crazy about her. He was never going to be another Andre Agassi, but his confidence was soaring.

Good for him, I thought. *And good for Mattie Lynn.*

BABE'S BLOG

My life is settling into a weirdly happy routine. For some people the word routine is anything but happy, but to me it's always good. It means stability. Not moving to somewhere new. And now it also means something else.

Zat, every single night.

Every night I search for him in my dreams. I don't plan it that way but my dreams automatically begin with thoughts of him.

Sometimes I see him sitting in a chair in the corner of a room, quietly observing the movie playing inside my head—for isn't that what dreams are?

My dead grandma might show up, or an old friend from middle school. Occasionally, I introduce the supporting actors of my dreams to Zat and he stands up and joins us, always happy to get to know them, to talk to them.

Mom and Dad love Zat, even though they don't know him in the waking world.

"Why don't you bring him around more often?" Mom asks one day when our entire family, including my brothers, are inexplicably living in the middle of a department store.

Dad, who's barbecuing while the department store customers gawk at us, suggests having him over for dinner that night.

"He's always full of interesting ideas," Dad says. "That boy comes up with things I've never thought about in exactly the way he presents them. Don't know what it is about him but you could do worse, Babe."

When Zat and I climb under the covers of my bed after dinner that night, we're careful to stay on opposite sides. We keep looking at each other and I'm conscious of every move he makes, even when I try to turn away from him (though that doesn't last long). We're in the middle of the bedroom furniture department and the store seems to be open 24/7.

At times, things are even more awkward. Once Perry shows up and is stubbornly arguing with me before breaking down in tears. I turn to look at Zat, half hidden by a shadow, but he shakes his head and puts a finger to his lips so I know not to speak to him while Perry is there.

"I feel for him," he says later. "He's obviously in love with you."

I learn that the less intense my dreams of Zat, the less intense my headaches upon awakening. But I'd gladly accept a violent headache if it means getting closer to Zat, although it's always a frightening experience.

Mai's the other half of the best part of my new life. We're so different and yet so much alike. We talk to each other about everything, or almost everything. I never mention Zat; I'm not sure how she'll react. I don't want to lose the one best friend I have in the waking world. Because of Zat, I also never tell her about my blog. I'll always be grateful to Earl for steering me to the fish market on that day, which feels like a long time ago, at least in *my* world where a long time is measured in months, sometimes weeks. We hang out a lot at the beach, mostly at night when neither of us have to work.

I love the honky tonk atmosphere of the two-lane highway that runs alongside the beach in Sugar Dunes. Traffic slows to a crawl during the summer months, everyone trying to get their fill of everything the glittering gulf has to offer. The craziest miniature golf courses you've ever seen. Water parks, sea life aquariums, huge beachwear markets, and southern style fast food. All of it is endlessly fascinating to me but so ordinary for Mai. But she's always up for checking out places she's probably been to a thousand times before.

Comments:

Sweetness: but is this still the dream or was perry really there? i feel for him too so i'm glad he didn't know zat was hiding although maybe zat shouldn't have been spying on your argument with perry.

Babe: It's in my dream so I have no control over what happens, and Zat exists in my dreams so it's not exactly like he can leave if I'm the one who's creating him.

Sandman: Hey y'all. How r u doing Sweetness and Babe? Ever make it to the beach on the weekends? Maybe we can all meet up or something

Babe: Ya, maybe. Sometime. I'm busy a lot on the weekends with work.

These50States: Hi there. I'm a friend of RoadWarrior's and she mentioned your blog. Could you give me some suggestions for a nice place to get great seafood? We'll be coming down in November for the first time. We're newly retired snowbirds from Canada. I'll check back later.

Babe: I actually haven't been to any fancy places but I can ask my friend and if she has any suggestions I'll post it next time.

RoadWarrior: Did you ever get your headaches checked out, dear? I'm very worried about you. Make sure to tell the doctor about your recurring dreams too.

Babe: I'm fine. I'm good. Thanks for your concern.

DreamMe: Trust Mai.

Babe: I do. What do you mean?

DreamMe: Do you?

ZAT

He was worried. Would he ever understand these people? Babe wasn't always forthcoming about the events in her life. Not that she was trying to deceive him, but the way the human mind functioned in dreams didn't guarantee that relevant issues would always surface. No wonder the brain had adapted over all those years to eliminate the necessity for dreaming. The idea was so intriguing that, just once, he wished he could experience a real dream, although he cherished the simple dreams he'd had of Babe.

He was learning to interpret Babe's dreams and their larger significance. For instance, recently she dreamed of falling down a staircase and of course he was there to catch her. But why had she dreamed about this? Something was bothering her, but what? And how could he help her if she didn't tell him?

When he asked her about it, she admitted to a disturbing event with an older man named Mr. Buell. This was something Zat would never be able to understand. That type of behavior was cause for expulsion from his community. No one would even consider it. Perhaps his peers could be indifferent to each other at times, but one would never cruelly impose his power over another.

There was so much he had to learn. Small things he couldn't possibly have absorbed during his investigation of life in this place and this time. He had to go slowly and let Babe show him the way. He couldn't impose his standards on her. He could only be there to help to the extent it was possible.

He wished it could be so much more.

Nine

Alonso and LeGrand were together again. I wasn't sure if it was a good thing or a bad thing. I also wasn't sure why LeGrand even bothered with the program, he seemed so genuinely uninterested. With his family contacts, I was pretty sure he didn't have to worry about getting into the college of his choice. He probably had a spot reserved for him at Yale or Princeton or Duke, something that came along with a generous donation from his father to the school of LeGrand's choice. But when I thought about it, Alonso and LeGrand were the perfect match—both equally contemptuous of the Friends Across the Bay program.

At the beginning of the second week, Alonso showed up with his ankle wrapped with a compression bandage, claiming an injury, which I seriously doubted. It seemed to suit both of them just fine. They spent a lot of time in the tennis clubhouse with me serving them cokes that LeGrand signed for on his father's account. They didn't exactly have deep conversations, but they seemed to be having fun.

In a strange way, those times the three of us spent together helped to create a bond. And somewhere along the way, the bond turned into an actual friendship. LeGrand asked a lot of questions about life in California, almost fixated on the subject. I told him what I knew about the real California—life and the people outside the country club gates. If he wanted to know about country club living, he had to look no further than Crystal Point. He asked me if I surfed (which I didn't). If Californians did a lot of drugs (no more than anywhere else from what I could tell). If everyone there was a vegetarian and a hippie. He was pleased to learn I was a former vegetarian, confirming at least one of his California stereotypes. The fact that I'd lapsed after moving to Florida only reinforced it in his mind.

"If you only eat vegetables, you'll turn into a vegetable," he warned me.

"So what happens if I only eat animals?" I came back at him.

"You'll be an animal," Alonso said with downcast eyes and a wicked grin.

LeGrand laughed so hard, I had to join in. It was unusual, but gratifying, to see Alonso come out of his shell around us.

LeGrand was funny and entertained us with crazy stories about his world in the sheltered South of the uber wealthy. He rarely had anything nice to say about it, but at the same time he definitely took advantage of all the perks that came with it.

"Walk away if it's so terrible," I only half-kidded him. This was on a day when he'd just bought the most expensive tennis racket we carried—signed for, of course, using his dad's account.

"Maybe I will one day." It was the only time I ever saw the little smirk disappear from his face. But I knew he'd never walk away. People who get used to money don't know what to do without it.

Alonso was a good listener but still too shy to participate much in conversations that included me, a girl. He didn't have an eye contact problem with LeGrand, but he never looked me directly in the eye, not even once.

One day, after I shooed them out of the clubhouse claiming there were things they could work on even with Alonso's taped ankle, they dragged two chairs out on either side of the net and playfully hit the ball back and forth until Mattie Lynn yelled at them to get the chairs off the court and go home if they couldn't think of anything better to do. I was glad she did it because otherwise I would have had to put a stop to it myself. But I was happy for the company of LeGrand and Alonso. They made the time at work go by faster and distracted me from the frequent headaches which lasted longer and longer into the day. I hoped Alonso wasn't picking up on the smell of alcohol I frequently detected on LeGrand's breath, even though I didn't see how he could miss it.

I was living my days just for my nights.

BABE'S BLOG

Zat's there for me every night. I no longer have to find him; he always finds me. We sit together on the beach and watch the sunset light up the sky in a riot of pink and red swirls. We visit the giant redwood forests of California; icy cold Lake Tahoe with its crystal blue water, nestled in the Sierra Nevada mountain range; even the craggy red cliffs of the Grand Canyon that suck the breath from your lungs and make your heart pound. We watch the Fourth of July fireworks I once saw at the National Mall in Washington DC.

Whatever it is, wherever we go, Zat can't get enough. He wants to go somewhere new every night but when I ask him why we can't go someplace I've never been before, he doesn't answer.

The morning after our first kiss, I wake up in such horrific pain I'm sure I'll see a lump on my forehead when I look in the mirror. The pain is so awful I barely remember the kiss which preceded it—only that there was one. It occurs to me right then I might have a brain tumor. Maybe that explains the dreams, the crippling headaches. I burst into tears, sure that I'm dying when my mom walks in my room to wake me up for work.

"Baby!" she runs to my bed where I'm sobbing. "What's wrong?"

"I have an awful headache," I blubber. "I've been having them every day but this is the worst."

"Why didn't you say something before?"

"I don't know. They usually go away after a while."

"I'm going to call the doctor right now. See if they can get you in today."

I'm so convinced I'm dying, I agree to see the doctor. I'm also scared to death that somehow whatever the doctor does is going to be the end of me and Zat.

The doctor's a nice older guy who immediately puts me at ease. He asks a lot of questions about my family history. Does anyone in my family have migraines? Yes, my father did but he grew out of them. When did he start getting them? Around my age. When did he grow out of them? About five years ago although he still suffers from an occasional attack. The doctor does some neurological tests, making me follow his finger with my eyes and stand on one foot and some other stuff, before he pronounces that I'm most likely going to inherit Dad's migraines. He gives me medication so the headaches won't ruin my life, and I leave with a prescription to be filled if needed.

I'll bet nobody before has ever been so happy to get

the diagnosis of a lifetime of migraines. I'm not going to die *and* I get to keep Zat in my life!

That night I tell Zat about the headaches.

"Why didn't you tell me before, Babe?" Which is the same question Mom asked.

"The only thing that gets me through the day is looking forward to being with you at night. I didn't want to ruin things between us. And anyway, I never have a headache when I'm with you, only when I wake up."

Zat gets real quiet and the smile falls from his face.

"I'm doing this to you, Babe. It's my fault."

"Don't be ridiculous! You're what gets me through it. I just have migraines which run in my family."

But the next three nights, Zat doesn't come to me and I can't find him no matter where I look. Each morning I wake up, exhausted, discouraged, but free of any pain. I don't bother to fill my prescription. If headaches are the price I have to pay to be with Zat, I'll suffer in silence.

According to Mai, Captain Phillip's is a great restaurant where you can get fresh seafood year-round. It's supposedly a little expensive. I've never been there.

Comments:

Sweetness: okay, so i'm really bummed for you that you have to have these headaches for like your whole life. i get a headache sometimes when i'm having my period and that's bad enough. i can't imagine having them every day.

RoadWarrior: Oh, Babe! I'm so relieved to hear that although I know migraines can be a nasty business. I'm so happy to hear it was nothing more serious.

Babe: Thanks, guys. Now that I know what it is, I can deal with it.

These50States: Can't wait to try out Captain Phillip's. Look forward to seeing you come November, RoadWarrior!

DreamMe: from pain comes growth.

    Babe: Um . . . hopefully not the brain tumor type of growth.

        DreamMe: that's not what I meant

Ten

After the showdown with Mr. Buell, we were careful to avoid each other. I liked to think he'd been drinking too much that day and was ashamed of himself once he sobered up, although I wondered if he ever really sobered up. Whenever I saw him, he always had a dreamy alcoholic glaze in his eyes. There were lots of times when the Buells had Bloody Marys sent over from the main club, and after a few of those, Mrs. Buell would get this look like she was fantasizing about sticking a knife in her husband's back.

Because Mr. Buell kept his distance and because LeGrand and I were kind-of-sort-of friends, my guard was down the day I found myself alone with Mr. Buell once again. Bing was outside giving a lesson and I was on the laptop tallying up the stats for a tennis tournament, ongoing since the past week. I looked up when I heard the jingle bells of the opening door.

"Hey there, precious." Mr. Buell made his way over to me. I literally felt the tiny hairs on the back of my neck stand up.

"What can I help you with, sir?" The *sir* was not the friendly, informal kind Bing had taught me. It was more the, *okay you've got power over me and I don't like it* kind.

"Sir? We're beyond that by now, aren't we?"

I didn't say a word but just waited to see what would happen next. He got real close to me—so close our arms were touching. I stepped to the side a few inches and he reached around behind me and rubbed his hand up and down my back.

"Mr. Buell, could you stop? That's really inappropriate, and you're making me uncomfortable." I took another step away from him.

"Awww, now I don't wanna make you uncomfortable. You know Mrs. Buell and I think the world of you."

Why he brought his wife into this majorly disturbing moment, I wasn't sure. As though she was somehow giving him permission, so it was okay.

"If you think the world of me, like you say, you won't ever do that again." My face was hot with anger.

"Your daddy's the new golf pro, isn't he? Pat Fremont?"

"Yes, he is." I heard the threatening subtext of his question and my stomach sunk like a diving sub.

"I ran into him the other day. He's a real nice fella, by golly. Your mama too, pretty lady. I can see where you get your good looks."

Here was the threat. He didn't have to say it—put up

or shut up. How did I feel about another move to another state, if Dad could even find a job in this economy?

My mouth opened once or twice, all kinds of responses on the tip of my tongue. Then, just like the saying goes, I was saved by the bell. The door jingled open and Bing walked in. For a half second he seemed to be studying the expression on my face, and then he shifted his gaze to Mr. Buell.

"The court's open now, sir, if you're ready."

"Ready, willing, and able, Bing! Let's get to it." He turned and smiled so nice, you'd never know what a pig he really was. "Thanks for your help, Babe."

I reminded myself that in six weeks the Buells would get back on their boat and sail up the Mississippi River to Memphis where I would never have to see them again. I'd be leaving for college in a year, and the following summer I could find a job wherever I decided to go to school. All I had to do was try to avoid Mr. Buell for this one summer, and then I'd be done with him forever. In the meantime, I couldn't put my parents' future in jeopardy.

Why me? I didn't kid myself that I was irresistible to men. He would never pull this shit on someone like Mattie Lynn and, if young girls were his thing, she was definitely a much more attractive target. But no, it wasn't about that. I knew it was all about power for him, and I was a "nobody." It made me wonder about Kay who was on leave from the tennis shop. Had she experienced the same thing with Mr. Buell? And how much did Bing know, if anything? I had a lot of questions, but the most important one—how was I going to handle it?—I had no answer for that.

BABE'S BLOG

My parents pick up on my quietness the night I come home after another unpleasant encounter with an extra-special VIP at the club. Even though I try to force myself to talk about my day and act cheerful, I get tired of pretending so after dinner I tell them I'm tired. I explain it was a long day and I'd hit with a few people in the afternoon when it was really hot. They're excited for me, knowing how much I want to play, but it's a lie. I haven't hit with anyone since arriving at Crystal Point.

All I want to do is go to sleep and find Zat. I need someone who understands what I'm going through, but he's still missing, having disappeared from my dreams since I told him about the headaches. I know he's there—I can feel his presence—but he's deliberately hiding himself from me. It's reassuring to know that he hasn't left completely, but I miss him desperately.

I close the door to my bedroom and crank up the old clunker of an air conditioner, and then get out my blog journal to take some notes. After about thirty minutes all I've written is "I hate Mr. Buell," over and over again. I go on Crystal Point's website and sign in under Dad's name and click on "Member

Information." Mr. and Mrs. Buell turn out to be Clyde and Grace. I go back to my journal and write "I hate Clyde" about a hundred times.

I grab a book I've been reading and flip my pillow to the foot of the bed so I'm facing the picture on my wall—the photo of a café on the beach which first led me to Zat. It brings me peace—the place that never changes. If I part my lips just a bit I can taste the salt in the air. The sea is emerald green near the shore where white-peaked breakers collapse onto the snow white sand. Further out it's such a deep blue that even the bright cloudless sky isn't a match for its azure allure. Zat's out there somewhere. I just have to look harder . . . if I can only fall asleep.

As it turns out, I don't have to look at all.

I take a seat at one of the small tables at the beachside café. Zat sits down beside me. He seems as happy to see me as I am to see him. It's my first time there with him, my first time there at all. Before, I'd seen it only from the beach below.

"Where were you?" I ask. "I've missed you so much."

"I've been right here . . . thinking about you. Watching you. Wanting to speak, but afraid to."

"You should've said something. It's been hard without you. I needed someone to talk to."

He looks down at his hands, collecting his thoughts

for what he's about to say next.

"I can't keep hurting you, Babe. The headaches are my fault. There are things you don't know about me—things I should have told you by now."

"Is that why you came back?" The food that's appeared on the plate in front of me seems so unappetizing.

"I came back because I sensed you needed me. It wasn't an easy decision."

"Please don't ever disappear like that again. I can deal with the headaches."

I look down at the table and the food's now gone, although no waiter had been there.

"Babe, I should have told you this a long time ago . . . the day we met."

I feel a distance between us which translates to actual physical distance—the small table, no longer small. We lean forward to hear and be heard.

"Tell me *what*?" A cold fear grows inside me. What he's going to say has the potential to break my heart, I know that. Only his silence guarantees my happiness. "I don't need to know anything other than I want to be with you. I *choose* to be with you. And I know you want to be with me too. You said once you understood what it was like for Perry to love me."

"You don't choose to be with me, Babe."

"What do you mean? Of course I do."

"I chose you but you didn't choose me. When you know me, really know me, then you can say you chose me. But you don't know anything about me. You don't know where I'm from. You don't know about my life. You don't even know who I am."

My heart pounds. The fear squirms like a creature struggling to escape.

"Then tell me where you're from." It's the least scary of the questions and a way for me to prove I want to know him better. In reality, all I want to do is turn us away from the dark turn we're about to take.

"I'm from Earth, just like you."

I think this is strange. I don't tell people I'm from Earth. Maybe California. Or maybe Sugar Dunes now. But I let it pass because I'm afraid to go deeper.

"Do you want to know what they call me?" he asks.

"I know your name is Zat."

"I'm called Pioneer 675875826453829. My family, my friends, call me Zat. It means love."

But his beautiful eyes don't speak of love. They still observe me with a distance I can't ignore. Our table grows even longer and we're now about a body length apart from each other.

"Love," I cling to that promising word. "Why all those numbers? Why Pioneer?"

"That's my signature. The last real identity to mark my time on Earth."

None of this makes any sense to me, and his answers to my questions are doing nothing to bridge the gap growing both literally and figuratively between us.

"Where *is* your family? Let me meet them." It occurs to me only then I should have known this. Should have asked this question long ago. After all, Zat knows everyone in my family, even if they don't realize it. They'd all been present in my dreams at one time or another.

"You can't meet them," he says sadly. "Not now. Not ever."

Why can't it just be me and Zat? Why does there have to be more than that? But now I've come this far, I have to keep going. I have to know everything. Will it cost me? Will I lose him? My lip trembles and I start to cry.

"Please don't cry." He leans across the table, which shrinks back to its original size, and takes my hands in his own.

"Your family loves you. The name they gave you means love. Why can't I meet them? Are you afraid they won't like me?"

"They're gone now," his voice catches, "and I can't go back, not ever. My last day on Earth I was Pioneer 675875826453829. Now I just inhabit your dreams."

Still we hold onto each other, as if by letting go we'll spiral off into space.

"We belong to each other. *With* each other," I say. "Nothing else matters."

This is where we started, and although I know him only slightly more than when we began, it feels like we've narrowly avoided a disaster in our relationship. The ugly fear slithers back in its hole. My lunch reappears on its plate. A soft breeze ruffles my hair. Zat's hands over mine feel reassuring.

But I'm wrong. It's not over.

"And if you saw me for my true self?" he asks.

"Don't you remember everything that's happened between us? The day in the garden. Swimming with you in the ocean. Walking with you on the beach. Sharing you with my family, my friends. Haven't I already seen your true self?"

He hangs his head, whether in sorrow or shame I'm not sure. My hands are warm and then hot from a surge of energy which passes from him into me. I want to see his eyes, to be reassured again, but he looks away. His hands grow thick and rough. They curl around mine like the roots of an ancient tree. His skin turns the color of amber. His nails morph into talons.

The fear so tightly coiled inside me rears up like a cobra. Using every bit of my strength, I force it back, push hard against its venom of terror and look directly into the face of my beautiful Zat.

His lidless, unblinking eyes stare back at me, their copper-colored irises revealing no emotion. Where moments before there had been a perfectly sculpted nose, now there's only a small pad of flesh punctured by two breathing holes. Scaly, amber skin covers the place where thick, luscious waves of hair had crowned his head. I see no ears, and where I expect to see a mouth with full sensual lips there's nothing but a small, dark slit.

"And if you saw me for my true self?" he repeats, his voice so soft and sad, a million light years away.

It's impossible for me to describe the absolute feeling of despair I have upon waking. The ache in my heart dwarfs the pain in my head. I care about Zat more than ever, but I haven't been able to convince him of that before we're forced apart by the cold indifference of my sleeping cycle. I close my eyes and lay still, frantically trying to get back to him but my heart pounds and sleep won't come.

How many people can see through the superficiality of what a person chooses to present, strip away all the layers, and come face to face with that person's most difficult truths? How many people can do this and still be able to sustain their absolute and unwavering devotion? *I* did this. I would declare to the world my unshakeable commitment to Zat if I could trust anyone to listen. But sadly, I can't say it to the one person who needs to hear it most, which is Zat. He revealed himself to me and by doing so he risked rejection and loss. All he held onto was the hope that if I really knew him, I would still choose him.

I pray he'll have faith in me until we see each other again.

Comments:

Sweetness: holy s**t !!! what is he?
RoadWarrior: Babe, are you okay?
DreamMe: His future is in your hands.

Eleven

I decided to take a chance with Mai. If she was going to be my best friend, then she'd better know what she was getting into. So when we met after work that day with only vague plans for what to do, I decided to open up to her. But after hearing the first words come out of my own mouth, I knew it wasn't going to be easy.

"Have you ever had a dream that felt so real, you couldn't stop thinking about it even when you woke up?"

Mai had been waiting for me at the tennis shop while I closed up. She'd never been through the gates of Crystal Point before and was curious to take a look around. I'd left word at the gatehouse, so Earl had waved her through.

"Sure. Who hasn't?"

"How about a dream that goes on and on every night?" I was leading her with baby steps.

"You mean like a recurring dream? I've had those—like this one dream where I'm driving a car and I come to a stoplight and step on the brake but the car keeps going. I've dreamt that a bunch of times."

"I mean more like a dream where you might meet someone, and then that person shows up every night and you develop a kind of relationship with him."

I was pretty sure other people didn't have dreams like that but you never know unless you ask. Sometimes you think people won't understand an experience or thought you've had, and then one day you mention it and find out that it isn't uncommon. That's what I was hoping for, although I was prepared to be disappointed. Or even worse, embarrassed and ashamed.

"A relationship?" Mai looked at me a little suspiciously.

"It doesn't have to be a relationship. Maybe you just get to know that person really well, you know?"

"No. I don't know. Tell me about it."

"I didn't say it was happening to *me*." I could feel myself getting defensive, preparing to be ridiculed. Maybe this wasn't such a great idea. But then I remembered how Zat bared himself to me, and it made me a little braver about the whole thing.

"Hmm . . ." Mai said. "Somehow I had the feeling we *were* talking about you."

"Okay." I took a deep breath. "Okay, you're right I *was* talking about me. Just listen before you say anything. Hear me out."

And then I told her everything, and I have to say it felt pretty good.

"So that's it? Nothing else?" Mai asked. "You're not

leaving anything out, are you?"

Was this the part where she was going to recommend a shrink?

"That's it. Except . . . except I know the whole thing sounds crazy. And I know you're wondering how I can be so wrapped up in someone I hardly know, not to mention someone who doesn't technically exist. He's gorgeous, of course—up until the last time I saw him, when he looked like a lizard. But he understands me and respects me. He just *gets* me. I don't know how else to explain it."

"Babe. I think you need a boyfriend. A real one, not a dream boy."

"Okay, I didn't expect you to believe me. Fair enough."

"What about that LeGrand guy you told me about? Rich, handsome."

"I'm not interested in someone else's money, Nuggins. I thought you knew me better than that by now."

"Okay, what about the guy you left behind in California? Seems like *he* got you."

"It's different. Perry's a great guy but I don't have feelings for him. I can't even explain what it's like just to touch Zat's hand. We don't have to say a word when we're together. It's like I've known him my whole life."

"Sounds like a brother to me, someone you've known your whole life."

"Let's drop it, Mai. I don't even understand it myself, so why should you? What do you want to do tonight?"

"Show me around!" Mai jumped up and down, playfully clapping her hands, mimicking a small child. "I want to see how the rich people live."

A shiny black Mercedes sedan rolled by. The passenger,

a young woman with tumbling locks of golden hair, stretched forward against her seatbelt to get a better view of something in her mirror. Mai shook her head in a gesture of mock sadness. "I hope she doesn't have a zit or something serious like that. Really? Friends Across the Bay? How can you stand it, Babe?"

"Welcome to my life since the day I was born. It's not so bad. You meet nice people too."

"I guess I can see why Kiet loves camp so much. His mom was over at our house last night, all bragging about how her baby's a big tennis stud now."

"I think Mattie Lynn might have something to do with why he loves camp so much."

"No doubt. So what are you going to show me first?"

"We can walk along the marina. When you're sick of that, we can drive around and look at some of the houses. Then I guess we can get something to eat at the beach if you want."

"Cool," Mai said as we strolled off in the direction of the marina.

I could tell Mai was impressed with the yachts. Nobody could help but be impressed even if they hated the lifestyle the way Mai did.

"And the Empire State Building up ahead? Which CEO or movie star owns that one?"

"That's *The Lucky Lady*. LeGrand's boat, or rather his parents'."

"Oooh! Let's go check it out." Which of course we were going to do, since we were headed in that direction and you couldn't exactly avoid walking by it.

It was early evening and some of the boats were coming in after a day of fishing and island hopping. A giant ice box had been lowered onto the dock by a ship's crew. As we walked by a vibrant splash of color inside caught my eye and I stopped to examine the contents of the box—exquisite pink fish, stacked like pancakes, their bodies sliding and spilling over each other in a way that reminded me of petals on an exotic flower. Only their gaping mouths and their glassy stares were reminders of death. I felt a sudden shame for abandoning my vegetarianism. One of them twitched and gasped for air.

"Nice looking snapper," Mai looked at them approvingly.

"I'd rather see them swimming in the ocean. They look so sad."

"C'mon, Babe, they're not sad, they're dead. How do you think we get the seafood you eat? You think they all swim into the market and volunteer to be eaten?"

"Look at that one. It's still alive."

Mai picked up a hammer from a toolbox set near the ice chest and thumped the fish right on top of his head, extinguishing the spark that was once its life.

"Hey, what are you girls doing?" A deckhand called out from the boat.

"Just putting the fish out of its misery, sir," Mai called back in her sweet customer service voice.

"Okay, we don't need you to do that. Thank you just the same."

"I guess we don't look like Crystal Point residents to him," she muttered as we walked away.

But I was grateful to Mai for doing what she did, even though it had shocked me at first.

As we approached *The Lucky Lady* I could see LeGrand on the side deck leaning over the rail with a drink in one hand. As soon as he spotted us, he walked over to the front deck, right above where we would be passing by.

"Ahoy there, mateys!" He tipped his drink toward us as though he was making a toast.

"Who's Popeye?" Mai whispered to me.

"Hi LeGrand!"

"That's LeGrand?" Mai whispered again. "*Hot!*"

"Climb aboard," he said.

Mai looked up at him and smiled.

"Actually, we have to be somewhere," I said. The last thing I wanted to do was to run into Clyde Buell. "We have dinner reservations."

Which we didn't. The kind of places where Mai and I ate never even heard of the word *reservation*, even though they were always unbelievably busy. Mai pinched the back of my arm.

"Ow!" I couldn't help myself. Thinking quickly, I bent over, "I have a pebble in my shoe."

"Let me help you." Mai stooped to angle her face close to mine. "What are you doing?" she hissed. "Let's go on board and take a look around."

"Remember the dirty old man I told you about— LeGrand's father."

"Uh oh. Sorry."

We played around with my shoe for a while and then both of us stood up at the same time, probably looking like a couple of idiots.

"Please." LeGrand was waiting patiently in the same spot, sipping his drink. "I'm so lonely because my parents are out for the night. Don't you feel sorry for me?" His ironic smile was so sexy, and yet so maddening.

"Maybe just for a second," I said when Mai bumped her shoulder against mine.

"Just stay and have dinner with me. Seriously."

"Yeah, we should do that Babe. I think we missed our *reservation* anyway and they probably already gave it to someone else."

"Okay, I guess you're right." I'd make her pay for this when it was all over.

Of course *The Lucky Lady* was spectacular, even more so on the inside. Hardwood floors and walls. Even the king-sized platform beds were made of hardwood with built in matching dressers. Every bedroom was made up to look like a luxury hotel room complete with fresh cut flowers. I half expected to find a chocolate on the pillow— of course I'd only heard about that kind of hotel; I'd never actually experienced one myself.

The bathrooms all had fluffy, white towels which were probably never touched by a human hand more than once before being replaced with a clean towel. There was a game room with foosball, billiards, and a huge high-def television. The living room where LeGrand took us for before-dinner drinks was completely encircled by windows that were probably spectacular out on the open sea. He plopped down on one part of a white leather sectional that formed with two others to make a conversation area. Mai and I sat opposite from him squeezed up against each other with yards of space on either end. We were both equally intimidated after the tour.

"What will you have to drink?" LeGrand asked. "I'm drinking a mint julep."

I had to control myself so I wouldn't laugh out loud. Mint julep seemed like a cheesy joke. But I'd wanted to taste one just to see what it was like. Just a sip.

"Mint julep? Doesn't that have alcohol in it?"

"Of course it does, Babe!" Mai, the jetsetter. "I'll have a Dr. Pepper," she added.

"Mint leaf, bourbon, sugar, and water," LeGrand said. "Care to try one?"

"I'll try one," I said. "But . . . your parents allow you to drink?"

"We're in international waters. Anything goes." When neither Mai or I responded, he added, "that was supposed to be a joke. But my parents don't care if I drink. They don't care what I do."

A young woman wearing a black polo shirt and a short, white skirt appeared out of nowhere, as though LeGrand had rung an invisible bell. She had the sun-kissed look of a person who spends a lot of time on a boat. I wondered whether Clyde had gotten his greasy palms on her, but she didn't look like the type who would take shit from anyone. Maybe he didn't play where he lived.

"Can I get you ladies something?" she asked.

"Thanks, Jessie. A Dr. Pepper for beautiful lady number one—I'm sorry, what was your name again?"

"Mai."

"But you can call her Nuggins," I laughed as Mai jabbed me with her elbow.

"Only Babe gets to call me that," she said.

"A Dr. Pepper for Mai and a mint julep for Babe."

"Got it. I'll be right back with your drinks."

"Excuse me," I said. "Could you also bring another Dr. Pepper, because I literally only want one sip of the mint julep."

"I'll just bring you a small one in that case." Jessie winked at me.

"Suit yourself," LeGrand said. "No parents spying on you here."

The mint julep tasted like what you'd expect bourbon, mint, and sugar to taste like. And one sip was more than enough for me.

After drinks we moved to the dining room for dinner. This room was also pretty awesome with more of the reddish-colored hardwood floors and walls, and a black stone table surrounded by a bunch of ultracomfortable white armchairs trimmed in black leather. I worried that I might spill something on my chair or the white area rug underneath the table, but, fortunately, that didn't happen.

The guy who served us dinner, a male version of Jessie, wore a short-sleeved black polo shirt with some nice white cargo shorts. Black polo tops and white bottoms, I guessed, were *The Lucky Lady* uniforms—very classy. Mai was clearly enjoying herself. It was obvious to me she liked LeGrand, the way she listened attentively to everything he said and laughed at all his jokes.

I wondered whether Mai felt like I did, a fraud, but I suspected she didn't. I was sure Jessie and our dinner server knew I was staff, just like them. They knew I didn't belong there, and I didn't want anyone to think I was trying to be someone I wasn't. All those years of country club living. The lines behind the gates of a country club are clearly drawn and everyone knows what side they belong on. Mai wasn't from our world, although hers was harder than mine. Mai wrote her own rules.

Nobody asked us what we wanted for dinner, they just started bringing in different courses, which were all incredible—soup, salad, actual fresh-tasting vegetables, and snapper fillets. I thought about the rosy-fleshed flowers of the sea we saw in the ice box, picked and waiting to be gutted and scaled.

After dessert, which was crème brûlée, we went up on the deck and watched ribbons of turquoise and pink sky peel off from the sun just before it slipped below the horizon. We sat on deck chairs and watched an owl glide in to settle somewhere high up on *The Lucky Lady* for the rest of the night. On that yacht, I wouldn't have been surprised if a rainbow suddenly appeared and curved over us from bow to stern. I knew money didn't buy happiness, but it was unbelievable what it did buy.

"So what do you think, Babe?"

"What?" My mind had been drifting. I'd had an amazing time, but now that it was dark my only thought was getting back to Zat and finishing what we started the night before.

"Do you want to stay for the party?" Mai was looking

at me like she really wanted to but couldn't say yes unless I agreed.

"You'll know a lot of the kids from tennis," LeGrand said. He was on his third drink since we got there. Who knows how many he'd had before? Anyway, he seemed to hold his liquor very well; apparently, he'd had a lot of practice.

"Umm, you mean like Mattie Lynn and her maidens-in-waiting?" I regretted those words as soon as they came out of my mouth. I'd better be careful about getting too comfortable around LeGrand and letting my guard down. It could cost me my job.

"On second thought," Mai said.

"Ladies, do I detect you have a problem with ML?"

"ML, now is it?" Mai half-snorted.

"No, no problem. I like her, she's a good kid." I kicked Mai's ankle with the side of my foot. The last thing I needed at the club was word getting out I didn't like Mattie Lynn.

"That's good, because I want you to know ML, or Mattie Lynn as you call her, is a great gal. A good and trusted friend of mine since we were practically babies." I noticed his drawl was just a little bit slower. More drawn out. He was getting that sentimental tone in his voice some drunk people have. "And I will not tolerate any unkind remarks against my ML."

I thought we'd really blown it. LeGrand's voice warbled like he was going to burst into tears at the thought of Mattie Lynn's halo slipping from her beautiful head. But then he took another sip of his drink and looked over at us with a wicked wink and that ironic smirk. We all burst out laughing and I was relieved, like I'd just been saved from something bad.

"How're you such good friends if you live in Memphis?" Mai asked. "I probably know her better than you."

Thankfully she'd dropped her snarky tone after my warning kick. Even though I got the idea LeGrand wasn't awed by Mattie Lynn the way everyone else was, I suspected they were close on some personal level.

"We play a lot of tennis every summer. And we text occasionally during the school year. Facebook . . ." LeGrand sounded like he was reconsidering how well he did know Mattie Lynn. He had a hesitant look on his face as though he had just been confronted with a fact which put in doubt everything he'd always believed to be true.

"Anyway, we seriously wish we could stay but, unfortunately, I told my parents I'd be home early tonight. My mom needs help—"

"Wallpapering the kitchen," Mai interjected. I guess she didn't trust me to come up with a good enough excuse. "And I promised I'd help them."

LeGrand held his glass up to eye level and chuckled at it as though he was sharing a private joke with his drink.

"Well, I guess I'll see you tomorrow then, at Friends Across the Bay."

"Friends Across the Bay," Mai repeated. "Such great community outreach." She really couldn't resist and I knew I'd better get her out of there fast.

"Thanks again for dinner!"

"Thank you, ladies," LeGrand stood up and bowed, "for your companionship." I thought he was going to fall forward for a minute, but he caught himself.

And just as we made our way down the ramp, who should be waiting to board but Mattie Lynn and about ten or fifteen other kids, some of whom I recognized from tennis.

"Mai, so good to see yewww! How have you been this summer? Babe, are you leaving already? Won't you stay?"

To her credit, you could totally believe she wasn't surprised to see us there and was disappointed to see us go. But then again, maybe she thought we were delivering fish or something.

And all I could think about was the last time I saw Zat.

Twelve

That night I slept sporadically. I flopped around on my bed like a dying snapper in a bed of ice, but I didn't feel like I was in any bed of ice. Even with the AC roaring away I woke up a few times so drenched with sweat I finally pointed the vents of the air conditioner downwards to hit me on the bed with its full frigid force. When I woke up, I couldn't remember any of my dreams. I wasn't sure if I'd seen Zat, but I seriously doubted it. No headache.

It was dark and rainy all day which fit pretty much with the gloom of my mood. When we drove through the gate that morning, Earl told my dad it was a good thing, we needed the rain. It's funny because it rained almost every afternoon, but apparently that wasn't enough. In California, it never rained during the summer and we didn't seem to need it. It made me think that nature gets greedy, like people. Whatever it gets used to, it always wants more.

The clubhouse was empty most of the day, so Bing took some time off in the morning and left me alone in case someone showed up. Of course, no one did, so I just read, wrote, and checked my email. Mai emailed me a "surprise" in the form of an attachment which I didn't want to open on the work computer. Her message said something about having a lot of time on her hands at work that day, with no customers coming in because of the rain.

And the real surprise was an email from Perry. He just wanted to know how I was doing and to let me know he was thinking of me. He'd been writing a lot and asked if I was doing the same. I immediately emailed him back, glad to have his friendship again, and hoping that's what he was really offering.

In the afternoon, only three *friends* showed up— Alonso, Kiet, and LaShawn. The others probably canceled because of the weather, but these three had their own reasons for showing up in spite of it. For Alonso, it was his mom. For Kiet, it was Mattie Lynn. And for LaShawn . . . well I think LaShawn just hoped he could still go out and play in the pouring rain. He clearly loved tennis, and he was a natural at it.

But the courts were too wet to play, so the mentors without friends went home. The rest of us sat inside, drank cokes, and watched videos of old tennis matches on the clubhouse television. At one point, Alonso fell asleep during the video, his head on the table. LeGrand looked like he was about to join him.

Mattie Lynn was so disgusted with LeGrand's inattention she threw a tennis ball at him and it bounced off the side of his head and rolled into a corner. It was the first truly spontaneous act I'd ever seen Mattie Lynn commit and it made me smile, although at that point I was identifying more with the nappers. I was right there with them after my sleepless night. The white noise of rain on the roof didn't help my alertness level either. Everything felt so heavy. The whole day was like that.

When I got home I went right to my computer to check Mai's surprise email attachment. I waited for the image to download and then opened the file. A beautiful drawing, which I could tell was Mai's artwork, filled my entire laptop screen. Unlike some of her other work I'd seen, this one was done in full color. A guy and a girl, their backs to the ocean, heads tilted toward each other with shy love in their eyes.

It didn't surprise me that Mai caught me so well on paper. She took everything in and was such a talented artist. But the way she drew Zat was what amazed me. I didn't realize how closely she was listening to the details of my crazy dreams. And I was astounded at how she could take my words and create such an awesome image. It wasn't just his looks that were exactly right on, it was the whole feel of Zat. She'd captured him perfectly.

But that wasn't all, even though it would have been

enough. Behind the two figures, where you'd expect to see a setting sun, a lizard boy rose from the ocean only visible above his waist. He stretched forward like Neptune across the waves with one twisted hand resting on Zat's shoulder and the other on mine, as though he was bringing us together and protecting us at the same time. The scaly amber skin and the reptilian features—it was just as I remembered the last time I saw Zat.

Seeing it all in front of me like that brought my dream to life. It made everything real for me. Dreaming about him, thinking about him, even talking about him to Mai, that was one thing. But seeing him with me, that was something else. I sat in front of the image for probably about twenty minutes. I didn't even know what I could say to Mai. Any words I had would be insignificant compared to the gift she'd given me. When my sleep-heavy eyelids blurred the picture in front of me, I loaded the glossy photo paper into the printer and pressed *PRINT*.

BABE'S BLOG

PIONEER ONE . . .

"I wasn't sure you'd be back."

"How could I not be back? It's *my* dream."

"But I wasn't sure you'd want to find me again."

"Were you here last night?"

"Yes, but . . . out of the way."

"I wanted to find you. I waited all day to find you. But I couldn't."

We're in a plain room with concrete walls, sitting in two folding metal chairs which face each other. There's nothing in the way of decoration—just a hanging exposed light bulb and a bare cement floor.

"I'm here now, so we can talk." Our voices echo slightly, boomeranging against the hard edges of the room. "I'm ready to answer all your questions." He doesn't make any movement to connect us physically the way he's done in the past. "There's much you need to know."

"Who *were* you the last time? I mean, what happened to make you look like that?"

"Were you scared when you saw me?"

"A little at first. But I got over it."

"What you saw was my true self, Babe. It's how I look when I . . . when I don't alter my appearance to fit with your standards."

"So, who *are* you? I thought you said you were from Earth."

I nervously look around the room for a distraction, something to minimize the seriousness of the situation. But it's nearly empty. Did Zat lead me there on purpose? I know this place—a storage room my family rented for a few months one of the last times we moved.

"I come from a future so far removed from your life, you'd have trouble even trying to imagine it. My Earth, our Earth, it's not the same planet you take for granted. It's as bare and stark as this room. It's hostile to life. The sun is so hot that humans had to adapt in order to survive. The way I looked the last time you saw me—that's how your descendants will look. I'm the norm, Babe. I'm considered to be physically pleasing."

"Are you alive now, or dead?"

"I live here now, but only through your grace and only in your dreams. Our species is dying. Millions each day."

"How did you get here?"

"Do you want the technical answer or the simple one?"

I think for a moment. He's thousands of years older than me, maybe millions. There's no way I'd understand his technical answer.

"The simple one."

"We've known how to travel back in time for a while. But only when the rate of deaths escalated and the end of our species was certain, only then did it become available to anyone who could afford it. Before that, it was restricted to a subclass of scientists, your equivalent of astronauts."

"Is your family rich?"

"No. Everything my family had was spent on getting us all out. I chose to go back in time, although most people left in search of new habitable planets beyond our solar system. My family left, but I chose this way. I wanted to see the Earth the way it was. A magical blue orb. Such a wonder."

"Your family left without you?"

"It's always been my choice. Most people lost confidence in this method, but I never did. It was worth the risk. *You* were worth the risk. My family tried to convince me to go with them but they knew in the end . . . I'd always been a dreamer, even though people don't dream in my time. Some, like my uncle, either refused to leave or couldn't afford it. Certain death in a world they understood was less frightening to them than the unknown. But I'm an Earthling and I couldn't imagine living anywhere else. When I was growing up I devoured the books and stories of how the Earth used to be. I wanted to see it for myself, even at my own peril. I'm sorry, yes, even at *your* own peril."

"So, why me? Why my dreams?"

"For years I planned my destination—I apologize for using that word when I talk about you, but I want to be honest. All the information from the past is implanted in us at birth. We can access it at will. Like you can access information on your computer about what happened in the era of dinosaurs. But ours is instantaneous. It's part of our thought process."

"But you haven't answered—why me?"

"This area had already been programmed—considered desirable because of its proximity to the sea. Others had tried to come here before me. You were here."

"So, that's it? I just happened to be here?"

"No, that's not the whole story. The truth is I selected you. I fell in love with your mind, your spirit, your strength. Your red hair. Once I got here, I couldn't imagine life without you. I considered thousands of others but something about you spoke to me and I could never get you out of my mind."

I desperately want to believe him because I've reached the point where I can't imagine life without

Zat.

"What's going to happen to us in the future, since you already know everything?"

"But I don't . . . know . . . that. And I probably shouldn't have told you this much. Any information you have now about the future will alter it in unpredictable ways, maybe even in more devastating ways than what I've just told you."

"What could be more devastating than the end of life on Earth?"

"It's so far into the future. There could be more immediate consequences."

"Then why tell me anything?"

"I can't keep using you—hijacking your dreams—without explaining everything. Without having your consent."

"And the only way for you to live is in my dreams?"

"It's an awful burden for you. If it's too much, I'll go."

"Go where?"

"I can become so inconspicuous that you'll never find me. Or I can remove myself entirely."

"How can you remove yourself?"

"It's like . . . it's the same as if you wanted to remove yourself."

"You mean suicide?"

"That's the word which comes closest. I can't explain it in a way you'd understand."

I feel sick to my stomach. I want nothing more than to spend time getting to know Zat even better. And yet, being one hundred percent responsible for someone's entire existence . . . he's right, it is an awful burden. Still, suicide, or whatever its equivalent is to him, is unthinkable.

"There was talk," he continues, "before I left, before we had time to get any proof, some people thought there have been successful transitions to corporealism. But no one actually knows. There's nothing beyond vague signals that it's anything more than theoretical. The signals could be anything—even random radio waves. And the transition was viewed as too dangerous to attempt. Certain death is what most experts said."

"Corporealism?"

"The transition to having a material state, like you. Instead of existing solely in your dreams."

"What kind of vague signals? Who do you think sent them?"

"The man who innovated time travel was given our greatest honor. He was known as Pioneer One. He was also the first one to travel like this, and those of us who followed him did it only on faith and hope. We trusted his vision and his science but we had no idea what to expect when we got there. *If* we got there."

"You mean he was the first to travel back in time?"

"That's right. Some people think he sent signals forward to let everyone know he'd made the journey safely and successfully. To encourage others to follow him and save themselves."

Zat looks at me almost apologetically. Of course I know this life isn't a real life in any sense of the word. I also know he struggles to convey his gratitude to me while at the same time expressing his fears and frustrations. I am, after all, his host.

"Anyway, he was willing to try—willing to die if it came to that." I can tell by the strong emotion in Zat's voice that Pioneer One is a man he places above all others. "His example gave me the courage to leave my family. But a lot of people called it fairy tale stuff, something to give us false hope. To avoid mass panic. They didn't believe that signals had been received from Pioneer One after he left. They didn't even believe that traveling back was possible. Even I didn't completely believe it myself until the first time I saw you. Only those who left Earth were given the title of Pioneer. The ones who stayed . . . they have the honor of being the last of the Earthlings."

"Do *you* believe Pioneer One made it?" I ask. "To corporealism?"

"I don't know what to believe," Zat says. "But he was right about time travel. I know that now. I just wish there was a way for me to let my family know I made it." He pauses. "There's something else. Another reason I came to this place."

"And what's that?"

"The signals which were received—if they were really signals and not just a lie the government spread to placate us—they came from here."

"From here?"

"From what you call Sugar Dunes, Florida."

"I've only been here less than a month. How did you know I'd be at the same place where the signals originated?"

But I already know the answer.

"I knew everything that happened. I knew you'd be coming here, Babe, long before you knew it yourself. Now do you understand why I said I chose you, but you didn't choose me?"

Comments:

Sweetness: wow, just wow. if ur making this up u have one helluva imagination.

> **Babe:** I've finally come to the conclusion I'm not crazy and all this stuff is real.

Mai: hi Babe. I got caught up on the blog and yes, you have my permission to use my real name and this is totally the most interesting thing to happen in Sugar Dunes in my lifetime, although I'm obviously not as convinced as you are.

Babe: ☺

DreamMe: If Pioneer One died transitioning to corporealism, he wouldn't have been able to send signals to the future.

   Babe: Good question.

   DreamMe: That was a statement, not a question.

Zat

This was it. This was his life. Had he chosen wisely?

Would he have been better off at this moment with Sahra and her family, or his own family, traveling to new worlds—maybe better worlds, better than Earth? But no, how could there be anything better than the blue and green orb with all of its faults? He had chosen wisely for himself, there wasn't any doubt. And nothing he'd ever experienced with Sahra had equaled the connection and admiration he already felt for Babe. The passion that stirred in him just from the sight of her. Who knew he could be moved this way by someone with her physical appearance?

And yet. And yet. With only the taste that he'd had, he wanted so much more. He longed to feel what she felt in the true world. He longed to make her his, *really* his.

To swim in a real ocean with her, with real water. To know the people in her life in such a way that they also knew him.

> *Two roads diverged in a yellow wood,*
> *And sorry I could not travel both*
> *And be one traveler, long I stood*
> *And looked down one as far as I could*

He had chosen, and he had chosen wisely. But had he come with the expectation of corporealism? Had he been greedy? Pioneer One made the transition, Zat believed that with all his heart. But how did he achieve it? Pioneer One was a man above all others in intellect. And for his destination, he had chosen another brilliant man, an academic rewarded with the highest honor of his time—the Nobel Prize. Did Pioneer One have help from his host? Of course not . . . he knew so much more than an academic from long ago. But how could Zat ever know enough to make the transition?

He couldn't.

This was his life as long as Babe allowed it.

He mustn't be greedy. He must be satisfied with whatever she permitted him to share.

He'd given her what she said she wanted, which was the truth. Now it was up to her to decide if she could handle that truth. In the meantime, he'd give her what she most needed. Time to decide.

This was the single most important moment of Zat's life. Perhaps even leading to the end of his life. He'd soon know where they would go from here. Maybe Babe would go it alone or maybe she'd invite him to continue on with her. Be part of her life. Be part of her dreams.

Whatever her decision, he was ready. He was glad it had come to this. At last he'd know for sure.

Thirteen

The sun was out again the next day and Bob and Dotty Sullivan were waiting at the door when we opened. They played some tennis then came in for coffee. Between customers they teased me about how they were going to fix me up with their grandson who lived in Wisconsin. I missed my grandparents, so it was nice having them around. It took my mind off the information overload I was still trying to process. At least for a few minutes.

Later that afternoon, Friends Across the Bay was back at it, even though Alonso and LeGrand spent most of their time leaning against the shady wall of the clubhouse with their knees propped up, spinning their rackets on the ground, and bouncing balls against the low stucco wall that separated the club from the courts. For someone who was supposed to be a good player, I'd never seen LeGrand actually hit in a real game or even in a rally. I wondered if Dee knew how Alonso spent his time in tennis camp. Or did she think he was out working up a good sweat and learning the finer points of the game?

The truth is I wasn't paying much attention to what people were saying or doing that day. All I could think about was the horrible catastrophe in store for mankind. The end of our world. I knew it was a long way off but I liked to think of Earth as always being around even if I wasn't.

Dad was in the middle of a lesson when I got off work and Mom was balancing out the register. I walked around thinking about everything and wondering what kind of future I could have with Zat. Did he already know the answer since he was *from* the future? But when he was alive in the future there was no Babe and Zat. It was too confusing for me and probably just as confusing for him even though he had the advantage of knowing a lot more than I did. By the time I got home, I felt like my head was going to explode from all the questions piling up—like a parking lot that said FULL, but still the cars keep driving in.

When my dad pulled the truck onto Trout Lane I noticed a strange car parked in the driveway, a red BMW.

"Pat, who's that?" We weren't used to unannounced company.

"A young fellow. Babe . . . friend of yours?"

LeGrand walked away from our front door where apparently he'd been ringing the bell of an empty house.

"That's LeGrand Buell. What's he doing here?" My face must have flushed crimson because it felt like a fire was raging.

"The Buells with the huge boat?" Mom was intrigued.

I practically jumped out of the truck before Dad came to a stop. LeGrand was leaning elegantly against the tree in our front yard, hands loosely tucked into his pants pockets.

As I got closer, his faint smile turned into a mischievous grin.

"Miss Fremont." He nodded at me and smiled sweetly, removing one pocketed hand to sweep back his blond-streaked Hollywood hair. "I hope you don't mind the intrusion. I was in the neighborhood and wondering if you'd care to join me for dinner."

By then my parents had caught up to me, although my dad was holding Mom back with a firm grip on her arm.

"Mom, Dad, this is LeGrand," I muttered.

"Pleased to meet you, ma'am. Sir." My mom was already in love before he even shook her hand.

My parents walked into the house, leaving the front door open for us to follow them in.

"So?" LeGrand raised his eyebrows.

"So what?"

"So, would you like to have dinner?"

I was still in my tennis dress, the same one I wore every day. I reminded myself about the non-fraterniza-tion rule where country club employees didn't mix with members. But we weren't at the club, we were at my house, so I guessed it would be okay. And by then I thought of LeGrand as a kind-of-sort-of friend. I was hoping he felt the same way.

"Sure. But I need to change out of these clothes."

"Of course you do. I'll wait outside."

"No, come in. I'll be quick."

I'd never been ashamed of who I was or where I came from but I found myself acutely uncomfortable the minute LeGrand stepped through my front door. What would he think of a house like mine? Had he ever even been inside one? But he quickly put me at ease as he chatted effortlessly with my parents while I went in my room to change.

I finished dressing and was just about to leave when I remembered a message I'd forgotten to give Bing about a last minute lesson booked for the following morning. Bing wasn't always there right at opening so I wanted to let him know. I also wanted to rescue LeGrand from Mom's prying questions.

"I gotta send Bing a quick email before we go. You can come see my room if you want."

While I was busy typing the email, LeGrand walked slowly around my tiny cubicle of a room as though he was exploring the Grand Canyon. He paused for a long time at my dresser where I realized he was staring at the printed-out picture Mai had drawn for me.

"Who's this . . . other than you? Or should I say, *what's* this?"

I pressed SEND and closed my laptop before looking over at the picture.

"Oh, Nuggins painted that. It's one of those fantasy anime type drawings. She's got a vivid imagination."

"Hmm," he looked at it for another few seconds before putting it down. "She's very talented. Why don't you call her and ask her to join us?"

"Great idea!" The thought of spending an evening alone with LeGrand was intimidating so I jumped at the chance to include Mai. I dialed her number hoping she'd pick up, which she did.

I'd smelled a whiff of alcohol on LeGrand's breath. Barely noticeable. I hoped my parents hadn't picked up on it too. "Why don't you drive? I probably shouldn't." LeGrand said. I was just about to suggest we take my dad's truck but driving the Beemer would definitely be more fun. LeGrand explained that his family left the car at Crystal Point year round.

"No problem. You probably don't know your way around the other side of the bay anyway. Have you ever been there?"

"Can't say I have," LeGrand pulled his seatbelt across his chest and pointed to the start button when it became obvious I was looking for a key and a hole to put it into. "Make sure your foot's on the brake or it won't start."

"So how did you find my house?" It was the question I'd been waiting to ask.

"Lots of folks at Crystal Point know where Pat Fremont, the golf pro, lives."

"And the ones who know are willing to share that information?" I was thinking about employee privacy issues and whether those even existed here.

"Let's just say someone who knows was willing to share the information with a charming scoundrel."

"And who would that someone be?"

But LeGrand wouldn't say.

I drove over the bridge and into the guts of Sugar Dunes, the part of the city where normal people lived and worked. LeGrand stared out the window at the long stretches of budget motels, car dealerships, and fast food restaurants. A dead basset hound had been dragged off the road and left half hanging over the sidewalk.

"Now that's a sight you don't see every day," LeGrand said thoughtfully and respectfully, almost as though he wished he *did* see sights like that every day.

I pulled into Nguyen's parking lot, which was empty since it was after hours. Mai's family lived in a house in back of the market which was even smaller than mine.

"Nguyen's," LeGrand said. Except what he said came out sounding more like *oowin's* which was pretty close to the way I heard Mai say it.

"How did you know how to pronounce it?"

"Our chef buys all our seafood here and that's how he says it. I've never seen it before, though. Is this where Mai lives?"

"This is her family's place."

"Small world." The perpetual half smile of his expanded into a grin of sudden delight. Like he'd just figured out the surprise ending of a movie a full thirty seconds before the plot twist is revealed.

"What's the joke? I feel left out."

"What joke?" He looked over at me, surprised.

"I don't know . . . that little smile you always have on your face. It's like you're thinking about a joke nobody else is in on."

"Sorry to disappoint you, Babe. It's just the way my mouth is shaped."

I laughed.

"But if I ever figure it out, I'll let you know," he said, the smile lifting the corners of his lips. "Any more questions?"

"Why do you drink so much?"

I'm not exactly sure where those words came from. For the first time since I'd known him, the line of his mouth went straight.

"How about you show me where Mai lives? She might be thinking we got lost."

Mai got the idea to go to an oyster bar for dinner and she knew just the right one. It couldn't have been the décor of the place that made it special. The neon light out front was spitting and hissing its dying breaths. Part of the sign had already gone dark, leaving a headless flamingo under a leafless palm tree. The most important word, *Oyster*, was still visibly spelled out in lime green, although barely. Its partner word *Shack* had gone the way of the flamingo's head.

The story inside was not much better. A formica-topped counter was the main gathering place, although there were a few tiny tables in a corner so dark that I couldn't tell if anyone was sitting there. Most of the fake red leather covers of the bar stools were partially split, white fibrous material protruding from the torn spots like gaping wounds. Too much pounding of too many butts over too many years.

"Princess Mai!" The huge bald guy behind the counter hollered out his greeting. "How's my girl?"

"Hey, Georgie. These are my friends Babe and LeGrand." And then to us she explained, "Summer's not oyster season but if there are any fresh oysters to be found, Georgie will have them."

"I think we can rustle something up for your friends," he winked at us. "You know what they say, any friend of Mai's . . ."

This was my first experience with raw oysters on the half shell. Spritzed with lime juice, dipped in a horseradish sauce, eaten with plenty of saltine crackers, and washed down with Dr. Pepper. Of course it doesn't hurt to finish up with a slice of Key Lime pie. And along with a whole lot of talking, that's exactly what went down that night at the Oyster Shack.

"So what's going on with the FAB program," Mai asked. "Is it still *FAB*ulous?" Mai was semi-obsessed with the program that really annoyed her.

Ever the loyal employee, I felt obligated to defend it once again. I knew LeGrand wouldn't.

"It's going well. Some of the kids are getting pretty good. And Kiet still loves it." I looked over at LeGrand. "Kiet's mom and Nuggin's mom are friends."

LeGrand tossed an oyster down his throat and chuckled. "Kiet's a trip," he murmured noncommittally.

"How about *your* friend, LeGrand?" Mai asked with a seriously sarcastic emphasis. "How's he doing?"

"He's not really all that interested," LeGrand didn't take the bait. "But he's a good dude."

"So what's *your* motivation for doing it?" Mai wouldn't stop. "I get Mattie Lynn's motivation and it has college essay written all over it."

I loved Mai's directness. It's part of what drew me to her in the first place, but at that moment I squirmed uncomfortably even though I knew LeGrand was a big boy and could handle himself just fine.

"*My* motivation? My motivation is ML asked me to do it. You'd have to ask her what her motivation is, but I suggest you don't jump to conclusions based on your preconceived notions about her."

LeGrand was getting tired. Maybe he'd had too much to drink before coming to my house, or maybe it was just the closeness of Georgie's Oyster Shack where only a fan blew the heat and humidity out the screened back door.

"Okay, fair enough," Mai said. "What do you think, Babe?"

"I think . . . I guess I just feel bad for Alonso. He so clearly doesn't want to be there and it seems like a waste of his time. As for Mattie Lynn, I think she might be a better person than you realize, Mai. She really seems to care for Kiet."

"Well, I haven't exactly spent any quality time with her." Mai looked like she was thinking hard about something. "Let's go kidnap Alonso right now and get to the bottom of this."

"Kidnap Alonso?"

"I don't really mean kidnap him. Let's the three of us go hang with him and spend some time getting to know him." I could tell Mai didn't want the night to end and might have been sensing LeGrand's waning energy.

"Number one," I said. "He doesn't make eye contact with me and doesn't even like to talk to me, so I doubt he'd open up to us."

"Does he talk to you?" Mai asked LeGrand.

"Yup," LeGrand said. "That's about all we do. But I wouldn't say we reveal any deep dark secrets to each other."

"Number two," I went on. "We have no idea where he lives."

"I could talk to him tomorrow, try to get a sense for if he'd like to hang out sometime," LeGrand said. "But for now I'd better get home. I'm about to fall asleep."

By the time we took Mai home, LeGrand was already nodding off, but he roused himself long enough to roll down his window as she walked toward her door.

"You're a gifted artist! Love the picture," he said.

She looked confused for a minute until she realized what picture he was talking about. She smiled and waved back at him, her black silky hair swallowed up by the black silky night.

Thankfully LeGrand didn't have far to go after we got to my house and he took over the driving.

He was a nice guy, I decided. Too bad his dad was such a jerk.

And too bad about his drinking thing, whatever that was all about.

BABE'S BLOG

Once upon a time, I'd gone to bed without a single serious thought. Sleep was something I took for granted, not something I consciously planned for or rushed into. It was something that happened to me when I got sleepy. At times, I even resisted it when it interfered with fun.

Now sleep is something I live for, as pathetic as that sounds. My days are just hours to get through so I can rush into my dreams and be reunited with Zat. But the funny thing is, the more I crave sleep, the less I get and last night was no different. The drone of my rickety air conditioner was unbearable after an hour of tossing and turning. Finally, I switched it off and opened my window to let in the soulful barking of the tiny green tree frogs. At some point after that I fell asleep at last.

AND I DREAM . . .

Zat's waiting impatiently. He's my prisoner, and my mental state on any given night determines his very existence.

"You have to relax," he says. "Don't fight it. Sleep is

just another part of the continuum of your waking life, so let it come to you naturally. You have to be receptive and if you're not in the REM sleep stage long enough, I can't make the connection."

He trails his fingers softly down the side of my face, and the peace that's missing in my wakefulness comes to me through this physical contact. At that moment, I swear I can smell sunshine on his skin and a salty sea breeze.

But after the initial high, my sadness returns along with the very real problems for which we have no answers.

"What do we do next?" I ask Zat.

"It's your decision to make. I've seen everything I ever wanted to see. I would be satisfied even if it ended now. The one thing I can't abide is your suffering, emotional or physical."

He leads me to a carpeted staircase and we walk down, down, down. The further we descend, the stronger it smells like chlorine. An indoor swimming pool. I hear the *ch, ch, ch* sound of a lawn sprinkler.

"I can't stop thinking about the Earth. *Our* Earth. I wish I didn't know how it ended."

"Haven't you always known our sun would eventually die? Didn't they teach you about red giants in school?" Zat seems genuinely perplexed I might not know this.

"It never seemed real. Of course I learned about it but the massive amount of time until it happened completely negated its reality. But you've bridged the time for me like a wormhole. It's not infinite and incomprehensible anymore. It almost seems like it's happening to me now."

We're riding in the back of a hay wagon, a ride I once took during a school field trip in second grade. My classmates surround us, giggling and squealing as the poor horse trudges along a path it takes multiple times a day. "Wormhole? I'm impressed. You *have* been learning about space and time," Zat says as my second grade crush, Marvin Topper, jumps off the side of the wagon to get to the biggest pumpkin in the patch before the other kids. "But I'm sorry for you," Zat smiles at Marvin's enthusiasm. "Ignorance really can be bliss, and I'm not saying that to be mean."

"Why's it so hot if the sun's dying? Wouldn't the opposite be true?"

We wait in the wagon while the other kids spread out in search of the perfect pumpkin. A little girl I don't recognize calls up to me to join her, but when I don't answer she scampers off.

"Before it dies, the core heats up. Oceans boil away, solar winds sweep across our atmosphere. And then one day . . ."

"Don't say it." My fingertips gently shush his lips. I can't bear to hear him describe what comes next. I remember learning about how the earth will eventually be sucked into that inferno, but it seemed like a story that had nothing to do with me.

Now it does.

"You know everything, don't you? Because of the chip?"

"Something like that," he says without enthusiasm. "I can access every word which has ever been written. But to make meaning of information, I have to live it, to experience it on my own. You have to do the same."

And then he takes my hand and we run. We run so fast and so easily, I haven't felt that same joyous physical abandon since I was a little girl. I look all around me and see blue mountains frosted with snow. I see a black pond, thick with algae, where egrets bend their graceful necks toward its stillness. I see fireflies light up a night sky. I see shaggy weeping willows and shimmering, whispering creeks. I feel gray gobs of clouds above me, pregnant with rain. And I smell the rich loamy soil beneath my feet where earthworms toil tirelessly in the dark.

And then I know what Zat meant. I have to fully inhabit this world, to love it and my place in it so much that the thought of losing it, even long after I die, is unthinkable. I have to do whatever I can to preserve and appreciate the splendor of the magical blue orb on which I live. I have to leave behind my memories for everyone who will come long after I'm gone and will never have the gifts I take for granted.

Only in their dreams.

Comments:

DreamMe: That magical blue orb still exists for you. Keep it magical. Keep it blue.

Babe: Who *are* you?

FOURTEEN

An epiphany is a wonderful thing but when real life intrudes, it can be hard to focus on the big picture. That's exactly what happened the next day when Clyde Buell walked through the door and transformed himself into a major buzz kill.

It was midday, lunch time, which was usually pretty quiet. Not only was it hot then, but people were busy eating and taking their early afternoon summer siestas. Bing had taken to leaving me on my own during lunch. He used the time to run errands and once a week he returned the favor and let me take off for a whole hour.

But that day Clyde strolled in acting like none of the bad stuff had ever happened between us.

"Was Bing expecting you?" I asked. I knew he wasn't. "He'll be back soon."

Clyde didn't have a partner in sight so I was wondering what was up.

"I'm waiting for a friend—expected he'd be here by now. We'll be using Court 5 if you could make sure no one else takes it."

Court 5 was a prized court at this time of day, being mostly in the shade of a row of silver maples. Of course Clyde assumed the court was his for the asking, and anyone who might have reserved it would naturally be bumped to a different court. Luckily, it was open.

I brought up the computer reservation program and typed Clyde's name into court 5. He was doing a whole bit about checking his watch and staring at the door like he expected Mr. X to walk in any moment. But I instinctively distrusted Clyde so I doubted Mr. X's existence until it was proven otherwise.

I wondered whether Clyde knew about my friendship with his son, but I didn't think so. They didn't seem like they shared a lot of personal info.

While all the phony acting was going on, he kept moving closer and closer until he was right by my side, right where all the bad stuff happened before and right where I didn't want him to be. I looked nervously through the window but there was no sign of Bing, or anyone else for that matter.

"Is there something I can help you with while you're waiting?" I asked, making direct eye contact in the hopes of getting him to back off a bit. It had the opposite effect.

"There could be," he said. "It depends on you."

And in a flash, he grabbed my ass and gave it a squeeze.

How much did I have to put up with to protect myself, my family? What if I hauled off and hit him? Would anyone believe me? I knew my parents would, but would anyone else? All those questions raced through my mind in a fraction of a second, the length of time it took me to weigh my options and arrive at my decision.

I chose safety. I chose security. I chose my mom and dad. I pushed his hand away firmly but not violently. I hated myself but, at the same time, I forgave myself. Clyde Buell was the one I really hated.

"That's not fair . . . what you're doing to me. And I don't know why you're doing it. It's not fair." Maybe reason or empathy could reach this man.

He smirked, and for a second I thought about LeGrand's little smile. But Clyde's smirk was cruel, whereas LeGrand's showed amusement, or maybe even puzzlement, about the world. There was no malice in LeGrand's smile, I knew that.

"I *can* be fair, if you give me a chance," he said just as the bells of the door jingled and Bing walked in.

"Mr. Buell, sir, I didn't know you'd be in. Waiting to hit some balls?"

"I tell you what Bing. Seems like the fella who was supposed to meet me isn't going to show up today. How about Babe, here, comes out and hits a few balls to loosen me up?"

Bing looked skeptical. He still had never seen me hit.

"You up to it, Babe?" he asked, somewhat nervously I thought.

Without a word, I turned and picked up my racket, which until now had sat uselessly behind the counter. I walked toward the door without so much as a backward glance.

"I'll see you out on Court 5."

It had been months since I last hit, but I was strong and athletic. I'd spent years developing the skills I learned in my childhood, so once we got started the hitting was effortless.

My satisfaction was quickly interrupted when Clyde pounced on a short ball and rushed the net. When I lobbed a return back, he crushed an overhead which hit me right at my feet. His fake grinning apology made my already steaming blood start to boil over.

I gathered my composure and, using precision ground strokes, I ran that old man around the court until he became so winded I almost felt sorry for him. Almost. When he couldn't take it anymore he lurched toward the bench, huffing and puffing. He collapsed on his butt, leaning forward with elbows resting on knees and chest heaving. It wasn't a pretty sight. He wiped his sweaty face with a towel from his bag and, still unable to speak, gulped down a bottle of water.

"Thanks for the warm up," he finally said once he caught his breath enough to speak.

I'd been thinking we were alone, but that was far from the truth. A lone, slow clapping sound came from the mini-bleachers, which were also shaded by the trees. I hadn't seen anyone there when we started, but at some point, LeGrand had arrived.

"Way to go, Dad!" he called out, continuing the steady

beat of his clap.

Clyde didn't look up or acknowledge his son's presence. After a minute, I left the court and walked back to the clubhouse. LeGrand followed me in.

The "warm up" did not escape Bing's notice either. He was standing just outside the door with his mouth hanging open.

"Did you see Babe play?" LeGrand asked him. "She smoked my dad." He seemed positively gleeful.

"Can I talk to you for a minute, Babe?" Bing said quietly. We stepped outside for some privacy. "You never told me you could play like that." He didn't seem real happy for me.

"You never asked."

"I asked you when you first started working and you said you were *alright*."

"I *am* alright."

"That's not the word I would have chosen." He got real quiet for a minute and then without making direct eye contact he said, "I'm afraid you may have stirred up a hornet's nest."

"Or maybe a fire ant nest?" I suggested unhelpfully. He didn't laugh.

"Why don't you take the rest of the week off, Babe?"

"Are you firing me?"

"No, I'm not firing you. I just want to give Mr. Buell a few days to cool down and see how he reacts."

"How will you manage by yourself?"

"I'll borrow someone from your dad's staff."

"And what am I supposed to say to my dad when he asks why?"

"Tell him . . . tell him you're taking a much deserved break."

"He won't believe that."

"Then tell him you're sick. I won't call for backup until tomorrow. I'll get here early to open."

"Do I go now?" A sob was rising in my throat. I pushed it back.

"Finish up the day," Bing said. "I doubt we'll see Buell back here today."

The rest of the day was pretty dreary for me—like I had a guillotine hanging over my neck and it was ready to drop any minute. Here I was, playing by the rules. I could have said something about what Clyde was up to, but I kept my mouth shut. I thought he might be man enough to settle this game of his on the court. And maybe he was. But Bing had intervened without giving me the chance to end it in a way where my parents held onto their jobs and I held onto my dignity. But of course, Bing didn't know about any of this, so what else could he do? All this stuff was just petty, stupid shit. Why me?

LeGrand had stopped by just to say hi because I guess we were buds. But even though he was thrilled at his father's humiliation, he knew it wasn't going to end happily ever after. He knew his dad well enough to realize that. But did he know his dad well enough to understand why I undertook that semi-suicidal mission?

After a few minutes, he left, saying he'd be back for Friends later in the day. I obviously didn't tell him what Bing had just said to me.

DREAM ME

I'd call in sick the next day.

After the Friends were done for the day, LeGrand told me he'd gotten Alonso's address. He'd suggested getting together sometime and Alonso had responded, not exactly enthusiastically, but he hadn't said no either. Naturally, LeGrand hadn't mentioned me and Mai tagging along. It was nice to see LeGrand engaged, and he didn't smell of alcohol that day, but none of it mattered much to me just then.

"I have his address in our files," I said gloomily. "They have to fill out a bunch of forms when they sign up for the program."

"But that's not right," LeGrand said, ignoring the fact he'd gotten my address immorally. "This way, I have it with his permission."

Right then, he reminded me of a little boy wanting approval for a job well done.

"Good work," I said with the last bit of enthusiasm I could fake.

Another late lesson for my dad after work, so I had time to kill when all I wanted to do was disappear from Crystal Point. I decided to work off some energy with another walk, this time heading toward the gate.

The clouds had been dark and noisy all afternoon but they kept rolling through, keeping things cool without getting anything wet. But my luck ran out right when I got to the gatehouse where, thankfully, Earl was still on duty. I ducked under the eave where I stood the first day I met him. We watched the sky split open, loosing rivers of water that were already puddling around my feet. Conversation was useless during storms like those. They were loud and demanding—nature's divas requiring your complete attention.

When, minutes later, the sky cleared up and the sun came out like nothing had happened, I told Earl I needed to get back to the golf shop. My dad's lesson would have been cancelled because of the rain and he was probably wondering where I was.

"Why don't we give your dad a call and have him pick you up here on his way out?" Earl suggested.

Duh. Silly me.

"I heard what happened," Earl said once I finished talking to my dad. "But don't you worry about it. You'll be back in a few days, I'm sure of that."

I knew Earl was on top of everything that happened in Crystal Point, but this was ridiculous. It was another painful reminder of how closely you had to guard your secrets when you worked behind the gates of a country club.

"Yeah, well . . ." I didn't know how to respond, not knowing how much Earl knew and who he'd heard it from.

"You weren't really planning a career in the tennis shop anyway, now were you?"

"Nah. Not really."

I crouched against the wall of the gatehouse trying to make myself inconspicuous to the cars entering and exiting. A silver Audi drove through the residents' gate and Earl smiled and waved it on.

"What career *are* you planning to pursue, if you don't mind my asking?" He looked at me meaningfully.

"I want to write books . . . to be an author." That actually had never occurred to me until just that moment, and I think it was more me wanting to have something to tell Earl. The truth was, I always assumed I'd be a tennis pro working in a country club in some random part of the country. But I didn't want Earl to know how much tennis meant to me. I didn't want his pity. "I know it's a long shot and the chances of success are against me," I added quickly.

"If that's what you want to do, then do it and don't think about success." It was nice to hear Earl's words of encouragement, even though I had the feeling he could see right through my deception. "You'll never fail if you never try, but you'll never be happy either."

Fifteen

That night I started in with the "I have a sore throat and my stomach hurts" bit. My parents believed me, and why wouldn't they? I never lied about being sick before. Well, maybe a few times when I was six years old in Arizona and two of my classmates pretty much planned all their days around making my life miserable.

My mom put her cheek up against mine, "No fever," she pronounced.

After dinner I went outside and sat on the back doorstep. There wasn't any view to speak of, but I'd learned something the night before. The pesky pines that fought their way up through nothing but sandy soil . . . they were scrappy fighters. Even the fire ants were a miracle of sorts, building sophisticated societies in places no other creature wanted to claim. Not even the most toxic chemicals could keep the fire ants down for long. And the sun. The sun that was setting now so I could only see its powdery pink residue through the pine needles. It was still our friend, our most precious ally in this world. I didn't want to think about a time when it would turn on mankind and become its worst enemy.

"A penny for your thoughts." I was so deep in my head I hadn't noticed my dad in the backyard.

"Trust me, they're not worth it. And I say that as someone who could use the money." I was trying to bring a little humor into the conversation but it backfired.

"I haven't been a great provider. Sorry, baby girl." Now I'd made my dad feel inadequate. Way to go, Babe.

"No, it's not that. It's other stuff I just don't feel like talking about right now."

"Perry?" At least he didn't know anything about Clyde yet.

"And more."

"You know I'm always a willing ear." My father seemed sad. He wanted to be relevant in my life and I wished I could help him out. But I couldn't tell him about Zat. Or Clyde Buell.

But I could tell Mai everything, and I did. Sometimes she'd try to talk her version of sense into me, but she never judged. In such a short time, she'd become the best friend I ever had.

The next day she gave me a second gift—an ink drawing this time. Me in an ultrashort tennis dress with a big B emblazoned on my chest (super hero style), hands on my hips, way over-developed thigh and bicep muscles. Lying facedown on the court in front of me was a man (presumably Clyde), my foot on his back; two tennis rackets at perpendicular angles to each other above his head like a grave marker. I couldn't (and didn't) leave this picture lying around. But every time I sneaked a peek, it brought a smile to my face.

My third day off from work, Mai and LeGrand showed up at my house with flowers. Of course, Mai knew the real reason I was home but she played along when LeGrand suggested they pay a visit and cheer me out of my sick bed. By then I'd already "recovered" from my "illness" and was planning to go back to work the next day. Bing sent me an email that afternoon giving me the all clear. Clyde Buell hadn't displayed any signs of complete ego failure. In fact, he even expressed concern for my well-being when Bing told him I was sick. Gag.

Somehow, at some point, LeGrand, Mai, and I became the three Musketeers, hanging out a lot together. This could easily have caused trouble for me with the other kids, but Mattie Lynn was the queen bee and the other girls took their cues from her. So far Mattie Lynn was playing it cool, even though she dropped any pretense of a personal interest in me. LeGrand's status gave me some protection, although once he was gone only Mai would have my back at Sugar Dunes High. But who was ever going to mess with me and Mai? We were the dynamic duo.

Still, at times I found myself feeling for Mattie Lynn.

LeGrand was a project she'd been working on her whole life and then all of a sudden, he was the project she was forced to abandon. But I didn't see LeGrand that way, I just thought he was fun and interesting. A nice guy to hang out with. But me, the real me? I was with Zat.

Kay came back from her extended leave. She was nice once we got used to each other. She was tough and you could tell things hadn't come easy to her. She was probably only in her thirties, but the hardness in her eyes, her tense, thin lips, and her old-fashioned, tight, permed hair made her look about twenty years older. I knew I had to let her reclaim her former second-in-command spot under Bing, so I stepped back. I asked her a lot of questions when I already knew the answers and let her stake out her territory. She was the kind of person you'd rather have as an ally than an enemy.

With her return, Bing and I could take actual lunch breaks and eat real food at a real table in the back room if we wanted. Or I could leave my air conditioned workplace and get outside to breathe real air for a few minutes. I knew her arrival meant I wasn't needed anymore, but they'd keep me on for the sake of my dad. Once school started, Bing said I could pick up hours after school and on the weekends as needed.

Bing started hitting with me almost on a daily basis, as we had time to do that now. I obviously wanted to play for the tennis team of my school, so being able to hit with the tennis pro was a huge plus. Clyde Buell kept his distance and minded his own business. He almost always came in with his wife after that awful day.

Friends Across the Bay was winding down, so Mai decided we needed to make our move with Alonso before it was over. We'd be going to the same school come fall, so she thought *we* (meaning LeGrand and me) owed Alonso some quality time. Her logic was that we'd spent half the summer with him and knew nothing more about him after all that time than we did the first day he walked through the door. The way I saw it, Alonso was probably counting the days until camp was over and he could get away from all of us. Like a prison sentence.

"Come on you guys, it will be *FAB*ulous," Mai needled us.

"What makes you think he's going to want to see us outside of tennis?" LeGrand wisely asked. "Isn't it bad enough he has to suffer with us those few hours a day?"

"It's not *us*, LeGrand, he just doesn't like tennis. At least I think it's not us. Come to think of it, he still hasn't looked me in the eye, but I know he likes you."

I had serious doubts about Mai's plan. She'd never met Alonso, but she liked stirring things up. Stirring people up and watching to see what would happen. She had a strong desire to push boundaries, maybe the result of spending her entire life in one small town. I had a much more laid back approach to life, which is why we made such a good pair.

Alonso's house wasn't far from Mai's in distance, only a few miles. But it was a world apart in other ways. Like most places I'd lived, there were all sorts of microcosms within the larger world of Sugar Dunes.

The houses in his neighborhood were neat, tidy, and small, but they were built precariously close to a busy street, with petite front lawns which provided hardly any buffer between the traffic and the homes. They looked older, built in the days when cars didn't travel so fast, and people didn't worry so much about a random car losing control and careening through their front door.

The fact that doors and windows were left open in most of the homes made me think they probably didn't have air conditioning. This presumably explained why so many people were enjoying the late afternoon from tiny front porches, visiting with neighbors so close that a normal conversational tone was all that was needed to be heard by the person in the next home.

Smells of dinner on stoves wafted out through windows, merging with others to create one giant intoxicating aroma. We passed a house where the sprinkler was running on the front lawn for the delight of a small group of children who ran happily through its mist.

I was suddenly ashamed to be in LeGrand's flashy red Beemer. It was too much in a place where people lived so modestly. It was too much in Mai's neighborhood, or even mine, for that matter. I looked at it now as a bad joke, not the fun, sporty machine I had viewed it as only minutes before. I kicked myself for not bringing my dad's truck instead.

We pulled up in front of Alonso's house and saw the white truck in the driveway, the one that said "Cummings' Emergency AC Repair." LeGrand and I argued for a minute about who should go knock on the door. I thought

I should because I'd met Alonso's mother. LeGrand thought he should because he knew Alonso better than I did. We finally agreed to go together and leave Mai in the car because we didn't want to overwhelm him. Mai wasn't happy about it, wanting to see for herself his initial reaction, but she accepted the majority rule.

The door opened immediately and there stood Dee Cummings, the first person to show me a kindness when I arrived in Sugar Dunes. She looked at me for a minute, as if she was trying to place me, perhaps remembering my face but not the context of it. Then I saw the light go on in her eyes.

"How're you doing?" she greeted me warmly. "Trout Lane, right? No problems with your air conditioner?" She glanced over at LeGrand, maybe trying to piece together his part of this puzzle.

"Hello Mrs. Cummings. Yes, it's me, Babe Fremont, and this is my friend, LeGrand Buell, Alonso's mentor partner in the tennis camp." I couldn't bring myself to refer to it as Friends Across the Bay. Every time I used that moniker now, I just heard Mai's sarcastic interpretation.

"Is everything okay?" Her wide eyes narrowed slightly with concern. "Alonso says he's had a great time. Learned a lot."

"Yes ma'am," LeGrand took over. "He's doing just fine. We came by to see if he'd like to join us for sort of a tennis camp dinner. Just the three of us, actually there's a fourth in the car."

Dee relaxed visibly. "That's very kind of you. Please come in." She stepped aside to make room for us to enter.

The temperature was about thirty degrees colder inside. I should have known the Cummings would have one of the few air-conditioned homes in the neighborhood.

"He's back in his workshop. Let me show you the way." Dee took us through a cozy front room which led directly into the kitchen and then through the back door.

"I'm sorry, ma'am, if we're interrupting your dinner hour. We should have called ahead." LeGrand kept up his patter.

"No, no. Not at all. I haven't even thought about dinner, to tell the truth. Just got home from work. I was thinking Alonso and I would go out and get something to eat, but if he goes with y'all, I think I'll just skip dinner. Had a big lunch." She chuckled softly.

Alonso's workshop was probably a garden shed at one point but it had been nicely redone with carpeting, wood panel walls, and a large window which let in plenty of light. There was a room air conditioner, so it was comfortably cool. A little television was mounted on the wall and the built-in shelves housed all kinds of expensive-looking tools and electronic equipment, neatly sorted from what I could tell. There was a wide counter where he appeared to be working on a project. He looked up, obviously a little more than surprised to see us. Dee went back in the house.

"Hey dude!" LeGrand acted like this visit was the most normal thing in the world. "Care to join us for dinner?"

There was no small talk leading up to the question. I guess he didn't want to give Alonso a chance to think up an excuse. In retrospect, I was glad LeGrand came to the door with me because I was pretty much not even a factor after reintroducing myself to Dee.

"Umm . . . Uh," I could see the wheels turning. "Let me ask my mom."

"No problem. We'll wait for you." But what we actually did was follow him back into the house to make sure he'd say yes. I really just followed LeGrand's lead.

"Ma, I—" he could hardly get two words out before Dee responded.

"Sure, you go on ahead and have a good time with your friends," she said.

Mai suggested Big Mama's Fish House where we stuffed ourselves with fried fish, chicken fried steak, green beans, ham with gravy, grits, mac and cheese, hush puppies, and pecan pie. The three Musketeers did most of the talking, but that wasn't surprising considering Alonso was in the company of two almost strangers and one complete stranger.

Just before we dropped him off at his house, Mai came up with the idea the four of us should have a picnic on Hurricane Island the following Sunday. Alonso didn't object. He didn't actually say he'd come with us, but since he didn't outright decline the invitation, we started thinking about the possibility of a fourth Musketeer.

BABE'S BLOG

Zat has dialed back on the intensity when we're together. I know he's doing it for my sake, so I can make a decision which isn't clouded by emotion. I'm grateful, but I also miss it.

He's determined to keep things real for me so I'll grow normally into the person I'm meant to be. Because of that, much of what we do together is similar to things I do with LeGrand and Mai. Friend stuff. Only since it's happening in my dreams, it's weird friend stuff. But I don't see Zat as just a friend.

Love? The word sometimes enters my mind but I'm not sure it's real. Once upon a time I wanted to believe I was in love with Perry, but somehow I never managed to convince myself. With Zat, it's different. It isn't something I intellectualize like I did with Perry. It just is. I can't imagine my world without him in it, however that has to be. If it has to be in my dreams and there's no other way, then I've decided that's the way it will be.

A while ago I had a frustration dream. It happened during the three days Bing grounded me from work.

In the dream, Mom was at a doctor's appointment and I was supposed to pick her up. I drove all over town, first stopping here, then stopping there, and the more I drove the more lost I became. I realized it was getting later and later, almost dark. Then I saw Zat standing on a street corner waving me down.

I stopped the car and he got in the backseat. He gave me some simple directions and within a few minutes I was pulling up to the doctor's office where my mom was waiting outside. She got in the front seat and I drove her home. That tense, helpless feeling of frustration disappeared.

Zat knew something was seriously bothering me but he didn't pressure me to talk about it after I briefly explained what happened. He told me that frustration dreams were a way of working things out, and he'd always be there to help in the only way he could.

Another time, I asked Zat why he could meet my family and friends but I couldn't meet his.

"We're in your dream, not mine," he reminded me. "And because you've never met my family, you can't dream about them."

It makes total sense, but I still wish I could dream about them and bring them together with Zat. I know how painfully lonely he is and how much he misses them. Mai's mother must have felt the same way when her parents put her on a boat, and she never saw them or her homeland again.

I have one question for Zat that takes a little courage-building before I finally get around to asking him.

"Did you have a girlfriend before you left?"

"I've never really *been* with any girl but you."

"So you never had a girlfriend before?" I'm not sure what *been* means to him and whether he's trying to get around my question.

"I was entered into the coupling pool before my travel plans were finalized. But as soon I was approved to leave, I withdrew my name."

"Coupling pool?"

"That's how we do it. We're matched according to a number of variables. The system works well enough. Love usually follows."

"Like a matchmaker?"

"I suppose you'd call it that. A big government bureaucratic matchmaker."

"Sounds romantic."

"It can lead to romance and, in most cases, it does. But I couldn't go through with it."

"So there *was* someone else?"

"There was someone I cared about, but not in the same way I care about you. She saved my life, so

I'll be eternally grateful for that. She's a wonderful person."

Suddenly I realize I don't want to know any more about this wonderful person, whoever she is or was or will be. I'm grateful to her for saving Zat's life, although it doesn't make a lot of sense since he's only alive in my dreams. Zat once said that ignorance is bliss. I'm thinking he might have a point.

And then he places one hand on my hip and the other on the small of my back. His eyes get huge and unfocused and he presses his lips gently against mine. He slides his hand up and grasps a handful of my hair, holding it against the back of my head to bring us closer still. We push into each other to prolong the kiss. To make it deeper and more satisfying.

The intensity he'd been dialing down . . . it got dialed up.

Way up.

He was my dream boy once again.

"Did I do it right?" he asks.

Comments:

Mai: Okay, I may not be able to continue reading this. Just sayin'. Okay I will, but I'm feeling a little icky about it—like I'm a peeping Tom creeper.
Sweetness: this is really beautiful and this is what i've been waiting to read although i would have

preferred it to be with perry.

    Mai: Perry? Eww. Gross.

        Sweetness: i totally ship perry and babe and ur new to this blog so maybe you should go back and read the old posts

            Mai: Ahem. Maybe you should go back and read them because I'm in the fricking blog and I think I know Babe better than you.

                Babe: Can you guys please not argue?

RoadWarrior: Hello, Babe. So glad to see you're still doing the creative writing. Please be sure to add more of the actual locale details because I think many people my age would like to see more of that. Then we can get the cute fantasy love story combined with actual real life helpful hints for traveling to your area. For instance, if you could include the names of more restaurants and places of interest I think my friends like These50States would be more likely to follow your otherwise delightful blog.

Zat

Once they called him a dreamer and he was always pleased with the label. None of them understood dreams more than theoretically, of course, but to him it implied something beyond the ordinary.

Now, the ordinary is what Zat craves. An ordinary life with Babe. But what was once ordinary to Zat is beyond his reach.

When she grows old, he wonders, will she continue to dream of herself as a young woman? Will he be eternally youthful in her dreams as she ages?

The human condition, he realizes, is uncertainty. Uncertainty layered upon uncertainty.

That's the beauty he sees and the beauty he seeks. There will never be an end to it. Not even after he's gone.

He no longer dreamed of storms, nor of women, nor of

great occurrences, nor of great fish, nor fights, nor contests of strength, nor of his wife. He only dreamed of places now and the lions on the beach.

He must remember to ask Babe if she's read this book.

Sixteen

The Four Musketeers were on our way to Hurricane Island. There used to be a lighthouse on the island, but during a major hurricane back in Civil War times it was destroyed and never rebuilt. Now it was just a pretty little island in the gulf with pristine white sand beaches littered with seashells. A perfect place to do nothing. No cell reception. No private boat docking. Just a white dome in the middle of a turquoise ocean. With sea oats sprouting from its crest, it reminded me of a balding man's head.

Normally, it would have been a day which brought lots of visitors to the island, but the bill fishing tournament was the main attraction that weekend. The whole town turned out to greet the sport-fishing boats as they came in with their catch. It was even covered on live TV. I couldn't understand the excitement of killing those magnificent spear-headed creatures. They were the wild stallions of the sea.

We boarded the water taxi to Hurricane Island and the captain waited an extra ten minutes to make sure no one else was coming. When we finally pulled away from the harbor, we were it—just the four of us plus the captain. Thirty minutes later he deposited us on the shore and told us he'd be back in four hours. I couldn't believe our good luck. We had the island to ourselves!

I'd volunteered for food duty, and spent the morning putting together PB&J sandwiches, roast chicken, carrot and celery sticks, sliced apples, and bottled water. Not exactly Big Mama's Fish House, but my West Coast-bred arteries needed a break. We'd all come prepared by wearing swimsuits under our clothes. I even brought along a sun umbrella that we wedged up against a sand dune.

It was a day of pure fun and, for the first time since Zat appeared in my life, I actually had no thought in my head other than what was happening around me right at that moment. We occupied the entire island like little kids who'd been left alone in a candy store. It only took thirty minutes to walk around the island and less than that if you went straight through the middle. We collected a bucketful of shells and we snorkeled and swam.

While we were eating our lunch, Mai came up with the idea we rename it Secret Island and anything we said to each other could never leave the island. It seemed like a silly but fun game so we went with it.

"Alright, what does everyone want to be and where do you want to go to college?" Mai asked. She turned to Alonso who hadn't been very talkative and said, "I know you're still young so you don't have to answer if you don't want to."

LeGrand went first, "Where do I *want* to go to college or where will I go to college?"

"Both," Mai said.

"Where I *want* to go to college is southern California—UCLA or USC. Where I *will* go to college is Princeton."

"How do you know that?" I asked. "Princeton's hard to get into, isn't it?" I had an idea, but I wanted to hear him say it.

"I've got the right genealogy. My great-grandfather, grandfather, father, my uncles . . . they all went to Princeton. My dad gives them a lot of money. It's like a family business."

"Why UCLA or USC?" Mai asked.

"I've always wanted to live in California. I'd like to work in the film industry, specifically acting, if you really want to know. I've only told this to one other person so y'all go ahead and laugh at me if you want." The corners of his lips pulled up as though he was getting a head start on us.

But which one of us was going to laugh at this gorgeous boy who oozed charisma and charm? It was almost impossible not to imagine him as a movie star.

"We're not laughing," Mai said. "So do it. Scared of your dad or something?"

"C'mon Nuggins, be nice," I said at the same time LeGrand flung a dried starfish at her, ninja style. "Better work on ditching the accent, LeGrand, if you want to be the next Brad Pitt."

"I think I can handle it. Okay, Miss Big Shot Mai, tell us about your plans," he said.

"UCLA is one of my schools," Mai said. "Any school in a big city far away from here is fine with me. And I've always thought I wanted to be a commercial artist, or something along those lines. You next." She looked at me.

"I don't know. Maybe a writer, maybe a tennis pro. I'll definitely be applying to some schools in California too but I still need to do a lot of research."

"Maybe you can get a tennis scholarship," LeGrand said. "You should've seen her kick my dad's ass on the court."

That topic still made me nervous. Mai knew the real truth about Clyde, but LeGrand didn't and I wasn't about to let him find out. But the closer we got as friends, the guiltier I felt about keeping the secret. He was always inviting us to *The Lucky Lady* and we were always declining. Even that day he'd offered to have one of his crew members drop us off at the island but Mai said she just loved the water taxi. He had to be wondering why.

"How about you, Alonso? Any ideas yet?"

Alonso lay stomach down on the towel, his head turned to one side. The sun had already dried us, and a thin white residue of salt was visible on his skin.

He stared at the large pink scalloped shell he was turning over and over in his hand. "I have an idea," he said to the shell.

"And that is?" LeGrand gently prodded.

"Materials science," he spoke so quietly we had to strain to hear him above the sound of the lapping waves. "I want to go to MIT, Stanford, Berkeley, or Northwestern."

"Holy shit!" Mai said. "What's material science?"

"*Materials* science," he corrected her, putting an emphasis on the plural of the first word. "It's the study of the structure of materials."

"What would you do?" LeGrand asked.

"Work on a hydrogen battery for cars. Design cheap, high efficiency solar cells. Create a better artificial heart valve. There are a million different things you can do with that degree."

He said it as if it was something as simple as reciting what he ate for breakfast. *Are you listening, Zat?* I wished he could have heard Alonso just then, but maybe they'd meet in one of my dreams.

"Wow, Alonso. I'm impressed. Really."

Mai was beaming at him. A sweet smile spread across Alonso's face.

"Yeah, really, man. That's cool. *Very* cool. A lot more cool than being an actor," LeGrand added.

"Hey, no putting yourself down on Secret Island," Mai said. "Next question . . . what's your biggest fear?"

"Becoming my dad," LeGrand didn't hesitate. "That one was easy."

"For me," Mai said, "it's getting stuck in this town for the rest of my life."

They both looked at me.

"My biggest fear . . . I don't know. I guess it's finding out I'm crazy. That things I think are true, really aren't." I knew Mai got my meaning by the look she gave me.

"What the hell is that supposed to mean?" LeGrand asked.

"I don't know. It sounds stupid, but that's it."

"No fair. You're being evasive."

Mai came to my rescue, "Your turn, Alonso, what are you most scared of?"

"Nah," he said. "Nothin'."

"You're scared of nothing?" her voice rose about three octaves. "Not even zombies?"

Alonso's back shook a little like he was laughing but he kept playing with the seashell in his hand and didn't say anything after that.

The four hours flew by and before we knew it, Alonso spotted the water taxi on the horizon. It was a day I knew I'd remember for the rest of my life, and I was reluctant to leave it behind. The security of close friends, the beauty of the natural world. I wanted everyone to have what I had at that moment. I couldn't wait to share it with Zat and hoped I could share in a tangible way. We packed up our stuff and sat on the beach to wait, all of us with our gazes fixed on the tiny boat that slowly got bigger with each passing minute.

"Hurricanes," Alonso said quietly. It came out of nowhere.

We turned to look at him. It was unusual for Alonso to volunteer a conversation starter.

"What about hurricanes?" I asked.

"That's what I'm afraid of . . . hurricanes."

"Why you scared of hurricanes?" Mai asked. "Ever been through one?"

"Katrina," Alonso said without turning his gaze from

the boat that had almost reached us by then. "Lost my granny then. After that, we left New Orleans and moved here." The surface of his soft, brown eyes turned shiny with just a hint of dampness clinging to the lower lashes.

LeGrand scooted a few inches closer to him and put his arm around Alonso's shoulder, giving it a few pats. "Sorry, man," he said. "That's tough."

Mattie Lynn made a big deal out of graduation day for the Friends Across the Bay program.

She ordered a huge cake from the clubhouse, which I picked up on my way to work. It was rectangular with green icing, white lines, and a miniature net that split the cake in half. Four tiny plastic players, with rackets held in various poses of play, were eternally frozen on the delicious tennis court. She thought of everything—both male and female players, both white and brown-skinned. At the feet of one of the players, a small round gob of yellow frosting was the ball that would never bounce up to be struck by a racket.

Mattie Lynn gave out certificates of completion to all the friends and certificates of appreciation to all the mentors.

She presented me with a certificate of special appreciation for someone "without whose valuable behind-the-scenes assistance, the program never could have been a success." It was kind of cute. I admit I'm susceptible to flattery.

I'd picked up green and white balloons that morning to decorate the tennis clubhouse. A big banner that said "Congratulations to Our FABulous Friends!" was stretched across the wall. I'd made the banner at my house following Mattie Lynn's instructions. Mai helped me with the design even though she claimed she had copyrighted FABulous and it was intended to be used only for sarcastic purposes.

Everyone seemed to have fun, even Alonso, who truly was celebrating the end of the program.

Kiet was quiet that afternoon, probably mourning the loss of Mattie Lynn from his life. And as though she sensed it, she was extra attentive to him and hugged him every chance she got.

LaShawn consulted with his mentor about tennis team in high school. They were lucky to have him and I knew I'd be seeing him on the courts in school. LaShawn was going to be a freshman, just like Alonso.

Afterward, LeGrand suggested we call up Mai and have her meet us at *The Lucky Lady* where the four of us, including Alonso, could celebrate with a graduation dinner. Alonso called his mom to see if it was alright, which, of course, it was. I knew Dee was happy to see him get out and socialize whenever the opportunity presented itself. But there was no way I was setting foot on that boat and taking the risk of running into Clyde.

"I have to go home for a while and help my mom with something," I said. LeGrand had heard this story before and his eyes narrowed with suspicion. "Could we just eat someplace on the beach? It'd be easier for me and Mai to get to the beach once I'm home, instead of coming all the way back here."

"Okay," I could hear the hurt in his voice but he was

too much a gentleman to press me. "Alonso, how about you come and hang out with me, and when Babe's done with whatever she has to do, we'll meet up with her and Mai at the beach."

I hurried off, burning with shame at my deceit. LeGrand was so excited to plan this night for us, and once again I'd ruined his plans with a lame excuse.

"I think you need to tell LeGrand why you never want to do anything on *The Lucky Lady*," Mai said as we pulled into the parking lot of the restaurant. "Otherwise, he'll sail off into the sunset at the end of the summer and wonder why his besties never wanted to come visit his cute, little dinghy."

"*Dinghy?*"

"It's not what you think, Babe. Don't go having any dirty thoughts. A dinghy is a boat."

I threw a stick of gum at her. "I know what a dinghy is." I parked my truck right next to LeGrand's Beemer.

The guys got out of the car, where they'd been waiting for us, and we all walked into the restaurant together.

"I've been thinking," Mai said after we ordered. "Since Alonso's the only one who's likely to be a success in life, we need to keep mentoring him even after we all graduate and go off to college."

Mai's statement stung a little even though I knew she was just playing around the way she always did. Not because I was hung up on success, and not because I doubted Alonso's future success. I just didn't want to be prejudged on what might happen in my future. And what *was* success anyway? Happiness? Money? To me, it was the first.

"Good idea," I said. "That is, if you want us to keep in touch, Alsonso. We'll be pros at applying to colleges by then."

"Yeah, our college counseling services suck," Mai said. "I can help you with all the financial aid stuff when you apply to college. I already had to figure that out by myself."

"Maybe you can help me with that too, Mai," I said.

"What can *I* do?" LeGrand had been quiet up to that point.

"You can . . . you can find out what connections your father has. You know, pull some strings," Mai laughed.

"Hah! Funny," LeGrand wasn't laughing and I could tell Mai had gone a little too far again.

Alonso looked up from the food he'd been pushing around his plate while we girls planned out his life.

"You could teach me how to play tennis," he looked directly at LeGrand.

"You're joking?" LeGrand said, the corner of his mouth pulling up into that half-smirk.

"I'm serious," Alonso said. "I always wanted to learn. I just didn't want to be part of Mattie Lynn's pity party."

"Babe should teach you then," LeGrand said, the seriousness of Alonso's statement sinking in. "She's a lot better player than me."

And then miracle of miracles, Alonso looked me right in the eye for the very first time.

"No offense, Babe," he spoke slowly. "But I'd rather learn from a dude."

Out of the corner of my eye, I saw LeGrand's

surprised smile and Mai's open mouth. We were all thinking the same thing. And we were all so happy.

I thought about LeGrand a lot that night and even introduced him to Zat in my dreams. It seemed impossible that LeGrand wasn't in on all of this, because it felt so real. When Zat and I climbed into LeGrand's red car, and drove through the streets of Alonso's neighborhood, we eventually realized LeGrand was no longer with us. I was glad because it gave me a chance to talk to Zat privately about the nagging guilt which dogged me when it came to my relationship with LeGrand. I didn't want there to be any hard feelings or misunderstandings between us when he went back to Memphis, but I was afraid there already were. Mai only reinforced my concerns. I knew she had a big old crush on LeGrand, which might have made her more sensitive to his feelings. But who didn't? He was a human magnet—even Zat admitted it.

Zat told me to be truthful with LeGrand. "Be gentle with him," Zat said. "Just like he'd be with you."

But how do you diplomatically tell your friend his dad is a perv and that's why you avoid meeting up at his place? It would be a huge test of our friendship, and one that terrified me, because I'd reached the now or never moment. If LeGrand couldn't accept it, it might mean we weren't meant to be friends. After all, I hadn't done anything wrong.

I texted him to get together after work and right off he asked me to meet him at *The Lucky Lady*. I suggested the tennis clubhouse instead. We could take a walk, I said. I knew whichever way the conversation went, I was going to miss LeGrand badly. He'd be going back to Memphis in a few weeks.

Seventeen

"I really need to talk to you," I dreaded what came next. "And I need to do it before you leave. I thought about emailing, but it's too private."

I kept my eyes straight in front of me even though LeGrand was by my side. I had to stay resolute so I didn't want to be sidetracked by one of his disarming smiles.

"I know," he said, the seriousness in his voice matching my own. We walked along the marina away from *The Lucky Lady*. The path would eventually take us to a long pier which ended in a tiny spit of sand in the bay, a mini island complete with its own private beach. "I've been waiting for this."

"You have?" I kicked myself for not bringing it up sooner. If he'd been waiting for it, then I'd been torturing myself for no reason.

"I mean . . . I knew you'd say something before I left."

"It's really been bumming me out, I have to admit. In fact, it's downright depressing."

"Is that so?" He looked surprised. "I thought, you being from California and all . . . I thought you'd be more accepting."

"Being from California would make me more accepting?" I must have flushed a hot shade of scarlet on the outside because I felt a hot shade of anger on the inside. "Are you crazy?"

There were a few seconds of painful silence and then we both just stopped walking and looked at each other.

"Are we talking about the same thing?" LeGrand broke the silence.

"What are *you* talking about?" I frantically replayed our conversation in my head. What had I just said to him? Was he thinking I was coming on to him? That's the *last* thing I would ever want LeGrand to think.

"I have a boyfriend," we both blurted out at the exact same moment. Then, "Wait . . ." and, "What?"

It was what they call a comedy of errors.

"I thought . . . I thought you were talking about my being gay," he mumbled uncharacteristically.

"Oh," I said meekly. "I didn't even know you were gay."

Another long silence.

"Whoops," LeGrand drew the word out into about three syllables. "I guess you do now." He smiled hopefully at me, eyebrows slightly raised. "I'm glad you do," he said hesitantly. It sounded more like a question.

"Me too." I rose up on my tiptoes and put my arms around his neck. He hugged me back and I realized we'd never touched each other before that moment. "Why would you think I'd care?"

"Because I haven't outed myself yet. Only my friend in Memphis—and now you."

"Your parents don't know?"

"Least of all them. Especially my dad."

"It's probably tough being an only child, huh? Not even a sibling to share with."

"I wasn't always an only child," he said. "I had a younger brother, but he drowned in a swimming pool when he was two and I was five."

"Oh, LeGrand, I didn't know that either. I'm so, so sorry."

"Yeah, me too. That's when my mom and dad stopped acting like we were a family. They both blamed each other, you know. Like who was supposed to be watching the kids at the party? Anyway, that happened a long time ago."

I put my arms around him again and rested my forehead against his chest. He hugged me back. Second time we ever touched each other.

"I'm so honored, LeGrand. Thanks for confiding in me. It's awesome that you trust me with this."

And it was awesome. To know LeGrand liked me for the person I was. I admit there had been times when I wondered if he only wanted to add Mai and me to his gang of adoring groupies. But that was settled once and for all. Right then I knew we'd always be friends, no matter where our lives took us.

We walked all the way down the pier and when we got to the end we sat on the miniature beach where tiny bay wavelets lapped against its shore.

"This was one of my favorite places to come when I was a kid," he said. "There are miniature seahorses that live in the sea grass. When I was little my mom used to wade out with me and we'd catch some and take them back to the boat. Then the next day we'd walk back here and let them go."

"*I* want to see one!" Miniature seahorses sounded positively magical.

"We don't have a net," he said. "But we can come back before I leave. I'll show you how to do it."

"Cool."

"But we have to let them go."

"Naturally."

"Babe?"

"Yeah?"

"What did you want to talk to me about?"

I'd almost forgotten the whole purpose of this walk. But it was such a momentous day for us, I didn't want to spoil it.

"Nothing. Seems stupid now in retrospect." It didn't, but I was grappling for a story which *would* seem stupid in retrospect.

"Come on, tell me."

"I was just going to ask you from a guy's point of view what you thought I should do about Perry." I couldn't remember the details of how I started the conversation and hoped LeGrand couldn't either. Or if he could, I hoped the Perry story would fit in somehow. I apologized to Perry in my head for lying about him so shamelessly.

"Perry? The dude who was your boyfriend in California?"

"Yep. He's been wanting us to get back together and—"

"So he's your boyfriend?"

"What? No—"

"But you said you had a boyfriend. Who were you talking about?"

"Well, I meant Perry."

"Babe, were you just using Perry to keep me at a distance? Did you think I was about to hit on you or something?"

"No!" I tried to sound indignant but I felt like a fool. Lies, lies, and more lies. I hadn't heard from Perry in weeks. And the last time I did, he never mentioned getting back together. I was being so deceitful, and LeGrand had been so brutally honest. I had to tell him the truth before he left. But not just then.

"I didn't know he was still in the picture. Thought you guys broke it off a while ago."

"Let's not talk about him right now. It seems stupid after what you just shared. Another day, okay?"

"Okay. But then we'll talk, got it? I want to help you if I can, and it's *not* stupid."

He reached over and put his arm around me and pulled me to his side. We snuggled like that for a minute but it wasn't easy for me. All of his beautiful male physical presence. I wanted Zat so much.

After a while we walked back down the long pier, taking our time as if neither of us wanted this moment to pass. Bending over the rail we looked down on silver schools of fish swimming around the pilings. Off in the distance, an egret seemed to miraculously walk on water in a place where the sand came up to just inches below its surface.

"Hey Babe, maybe that's the joke." LeGrand sounded sad.

"What joke?"

"Remember how you once accused me of thinking about a joke nobody else was in on. And I told you it was just the shape of my mouth?"

"Oh, yeah!" I laughed. "I remember."

"Maybe that's the joke. Everyone thinks my life is so fucking great. It's pretty funny if you think about it."

"That's not funny." I held his face in between my hands and looked right in his eyes. "Your life *is* fucking great. Or it will be once you own it."

"Maybe you're right. I hope you're right."

We held hands all the way back until we got to the marina. When he invited me on board *The Lucky Lady* for a drink, I didn't have the heart to refuse. And if Clyde was on board, at least he had the decency to stay away. When LeGrand poured himself a shot of straight vodka, I put my hand over his.

"Why are you doing this?"

Without even looking at me, he dumped the contents down the bar sink and poured himself a Dr. Pepper. Neither of us said another word about it.

Eighteen

The next day began like any other, until it took an ominous turn. The Buells came in with their regular doubles partners. After their game, they sat at their favorite table overlooking the courts and ordered lunch and Bloody Marys from the main clubhouse. The lunch went on for a couple hours and the drinks kept coming. Eventually, the waiter, who'd been shuttling back and forth, just left a pitcher of Bloody Marys in our refrigerator. He also left a bottle of Scotch the men had ordered.

At some point, the women left, and the men kept working on the Bloody Marys until the pitcher was empty. Then they started on the Scotch. It was the slow time of the afternoon when the Friends program used to be scheduled, so Bing took a break since no one was around. I felt safe enough, because Kay was back in the storage room taking inventory. I hadn't been alone with Clyde since the last horrible incident but he'd been behaving—or at least he'd been ignoring me, which was just fine as far as I was concerned.

After a while, I looked outside and noticed Clyde's friend had left but Clyde was still there sipping his Scotch. It occurred to me he must have a liver the size of a basketball.

From this point forward, I remember everything in slow motion though it probably only took three or four minutes from start to finish. Each time I'd been in the same place with Clyde was like a domino, one leaned against the next one, barely propping up its neighbor, barely avoiding total collapse. In the end all it took was the flick of a finger, or that last sip of Scotch, to bring the whole thing down.

I was folding shirts, the ones we sold. When customers check out our merchandise, they pull shirts from the shelves in order to look at colors and sizes. The next thing you know the area looks like someone's dirty laundry pile, so part of my job was refolding the shirts and stacking them according to size.

I knelt on the ground to pick up a shirt from the floor when I heard someone behind me. It was Clyde—I'd missed those jingling door bells. I stood up but he had me boxed in against the shelves where I was working in the back corner of the room.

"You're a little vixen, arn choo?" He was so drunk he couldn't contain all the spit in his mouth and I was getting hit with flying globs of it. "You know what a vixen is, don' cha?" I swear, he was almost slobbering.

Yeah, I knew. He wasn't the first idiot to point out the color resemblance of my hair to a fox's.

"You're drunk, Clyde."

"Oh! We're on a first name basis now?" He leaned against the shelf, using one hand for support, forcing me back even further. "You're a seductress . . . a little . . . *temptress*!" He was seriously slurring.

And then swooping in for the kill, his flabby lips pressed hard against mine, his red-faced, boozy breath invaded my lungs. I was in a bad position for a knee to the nuts but I had a free hand and I pulled it back as far as it would go before I let loose to make contact with his softly unprepared solar plexus. He deflated like the bag of wind he was. And sometime in the middle of that slow-motion moment—almost like in the movies—LeGrand walked into the shop.

"The *fuck* are you doing, Dad?!"

When Clyde wobbled around to face his son, LeGrand was waiting with a haymaker of his own. And even though I could never reenact it if I tried a thousand times, somehow, some way, I was able to intercept LeGrand and prevent him from taking the swing against his father he'd have to live with for the rest of his life.

"Are you okay, Babe?" He pulled me away from his father and put his body between us.

Clyde just stood there, sort of swaying. He was breathing pretty hard and his eyes went in and out of focus.

"I think you'd better leave now." I hadn't seen Kay who

must have stepped out from the inventory room when she heard the noise. She could just as easily have said those words to me, but she didn't. She said them to Clyde.

He swung around to look at Kay, mumbled something I didn't understand to LeGrand, and then sort of lurched out the door. That was the last I ever saw of him.

I had to extract a promise from LeGrand not to go after Clyde or do anything that might end up with my parents losing their jobs. He was furious, but once he calmed down he got it. He did tell me, though, that he'd be letting his mother know what happened. Not much I could do about that.

He left soon afterward to face what kind of hell, I couldn't imagine, but I knew it was going to be a lot worse than mine. Then when Bing came back, Kay sat him down and told him exactly what happened. I didn't expect everything to be wonderful going forward, but in my mind I'd already won. For that one moment, LeGrand and Kay had my back while I stood up to Clyde Buell. And I was the one who came out on top.

Bing suggested transferring me to the golf clubhouse where I could work with my parents. He even offered to lay me off if I wanted to file for unemployment.

"You tell me, Babe. How do you want me to handle this? I can go all the way with it if you want."

"What do you mean all the way?"

"To the board. I don't know exactly how the process works, but we can lodge a complaint, even though Buell heads up the board."

Bing looked miserable and I knew the predicament he was in. I knew the predicament my dad would be in too. Another job. Another move. Another high school before I even started this one. Even if I pursued action against Clyde Buell, with all the resources he had at his disposal, I knew it would be a long and painful process. I didn't want to expend any more negative energy on that man and, like Earl had once said, working in a tennis shop wasn't exactly my career goal. I could easily find another equivalent job.

"Summer's almost over," I finally said. "School's about to start. Let's just say this summer job has reached its natural conclusion."

When I told my parents that night they wanted to call the police and file charges against Clyde Buell.

"Just for once let me decide the course of my own life," I said, maybe a bit too loud. Maybe with a bit too much anger. "I don't want to move again. I want to finish high school in *this* place with *my* best friend. I'm strong, stronger than LeGrand. Stronger than a lot of people. You and Mom have always protected me, so for once, let me protect you."

They respected my decision, so we agreed to move on. If they decided to leave at the end of my school year, that would be up to them. They appreciated the logic of what I had to say, and I meant it. Every last word of it. But the main reason I put it behind me was simple. I wanted to protect LeGrand, who'd been so willing to protect me.

BABE'S BLOG

Zat is gone.

Last night he sat with me and we talked about everything. About the duality of my life. One girl. Two lives. But only one of those lives had a past, present, and future. And that was the problem. Zat said he was powerless to help me in my waking life, and I was powerless to help him in what remained of his.

"Once, I told you that even though I have access to every written word, I have to be able to live it on some level before I can understand it."

"I think it's the same for everyone," I say.

"The power of the written word," Zat says. "It allowed me to dream even after humans stopped dreaming."

We walk through a forest of tall, bristly pines where light sifts through branches, turning soft before splashing onto the ground around our feet.

"'Though nothing can bring back the hour of splendor in the grass, of glory in the flower; we will grieve not, rather find strength in what remains

241

behind.'"

"It's beautiful," I say. "Who wrote it?"

But before he can answer, the sky darkens and distant thunder grows loud and menacing. Zat puts a protective arm around my shoulder.

A shadow emerges between the drops of rain. It's Earl.

"Mind if I join you?" he says in a voice curiously devoid of a southern accent. "Until the storm passes, that is."

"Not at all," I say. "Come closer."

A huge yellow and green striped umbrella materializes in Zat's hand and he holds it above our heads. Earl ducks under it too.

"Earl, this is Zat—my boyfriend." It's the first time I've ever called him that.

"Pleased to meet you," Earl says. "Mind if I take a picture? It's a hobby of mine, you know."

Zat, who's usually exceptionally friendly when I introduce him to people from my life, stiffens and grows quiet. He observes Earl with great interest but says almost nothing. I'm a little embarrassed, even though I know Earl will know nothing of this encounter in the waking world. Still, it makes me wonder what it is about the man that changes Zat so dramatically from his usual sociable ways.

"That would be nice, Earl." More than anything I want a picture of Zat and me to hold onto. A real picture, not just a drawing. "Is it okay in the rain?"

"Not a problem," Earl pulls out a strange looking black box and takes a few steps backwards. "Look straight into the camera," he says.

"Look straight into the camera," is the last thing I hear.

And then everything goes black. I can't see, but I can feel Zat's arms around me and I can hear Earl's voice. *Look into the camera . . . Look into the camera.*

I'm dizzy.

I'm falling.

When I open my eyes, everything's bright. But now we're in a simple room with wood-paneled walls and a stone floor. A window frames a tangle of green, beyond which a snowy peak glistens in the sun. I'm sitting on a narrow bed, old-fashioned in appearance. Zat's head is on my lap. He's weak, maybe even sick. His body is covered with amber scales. His copper-colored eyes are moist. I hold him with one hand and stroke his hot, thorny back with the other.

"I was thinking about my sister," he says. "The last time I saw her."

"What's she like?"

"Like you, Babe. Smart, beautiful, full of life. I wish I could talk to her again." He sounds so helpless and I can hear the terror in his voice.

"I don't know what to do. Tell me what to do." I cry. I feel all of his pain and the burden of my responsibility. "Tell me how to help you. Show me how."

"You've done all you can, Babe. You've helped me enough, and now it's my turn to help *you*."

But I think I know what he means. Helping me means leaving me. Leaving me means dying.

"Don't leave, Zat. Please don't go," I'm sobbing uncontrollably. "I need you. What will I do without you?" I can barely get the words out.

"You'll never fail if you never try," his voice is so small, barely audible now. I lean closer to hear. My hair spills across his face like a shroud. "But you'll never be happy either."

When I wake it's dark but the tree frogs are silent, sensing now the arrival of breaking dawn. I have nowhere to go that day, no job, no plans with friends. My eyes ache from the strain of tears still damp on my cheeks. As warm as it is, I shiver from fear. I pull the sheet tightly around me and prepare to face the day.

With nothing to do and no transportation except the old bike, I stay in bed all day, only getting up and dressing minutes before I know my parents will be home. I don't want them to worry, but I can't focus on anything: not a book, not my computer, not even my blog. I think about texting Mai or LeGrand but I can't do that either. For a while, I even think about Skyping Perry. But I'm numb. It's an effort just to eat and pee.

That night I don't think I dream.

The next two days are more of the same and the nights are devoid of Zat. I know he isn't there anymore. In the past, I could always sense his presence even when I couldn't see him. But now I feel nothing.

I think back to the time when I was four years old. Mom was pregnant and I was hoping for a baby sister. One day my parents told me and my brothers that Mom hadn't felt the baby move for a while. She went to the hospital and when she came back she wasn't pregnant anymore. My baby sister was dead. That's how I feel. I can't feel Zat's movements anymore.

Zat is gone.

Comments:

Mai: Pick up your phone. Answer your texts. Answer your door, I know you're there. I'm going to tell your parents if you don't do something soon. I'm going to

come over tonight and cause a scene.
    Babe: Please just give me some time.
Sweetness: girl, i'm worried about you again

Nineteen

The next day I drove my parents to work. I didn't want to stay home one more day so I asked for the truck. I'd been ignoring LeGrand's and Mai's texts for three days by then. Maybe I'd go see them. Or maybe I wouldn't.

When I arrived at the Crystal Point entrance, I could barely stand to look at Earl. It just reminded me of my final night with Zat. I gave him a half-hearted wave as I drove through the gate and he looked at me meaningfully, but only waved back. I'm sure he knew what happened with Clyde Buell and didn't like it one bit.

As it turned out, I didn't go anywhere that day so the truck wasn't necessary. When I picked up my parents, I invented all kinds of stories about how I was keeping busy during the day, but I don't think they believed me.

After dinner, I knew I had to get out, but I didn't want

to talk to anyone. I just wanted to be alone.

On the beach.

With my thoughts.

So that's where I went.

And now, I stand staring out at the waves which are settling down for the night—sliding instead of pouncing onto the shore. A tiny crab runs across the top of my foot that is buried in the wet, white sand. The sun slips below the horizon. The moon stakes out her queenly domain.

When I was younger my dad used to sing a song to me . . .

> *"You are my sunshine,*
> *my only sunshine,*
> *you make me happy*
> *when skies are gray."*

When I got older I looked up the rest of the lyrics. I'd only known the refrain so I was surprised to find it was actually a song about heartache and loss. I think about it again. Like my relationship with Zat, I only saw the happiness, but it was built on a foundation of inevitable pain.

A pair of arms reach from behind me and wrap around my waist. For a second I have the crazy idea it's Zat, but I know he can't be here.

It's Mai.

Sympathy and kindness radiate from her eyes.

"Your parents said you went to the beach. I knew you'd be here." It's one of our favorite places to hang out. "Why are you avoiding me and LeGrand?"

"He's gone." She knows who I mean.

"How can you really be sure?"

"A few nights ago. It felt like someone stole my soul while I was sleeping. I felt him slip away."

"Maybe he'll come back?" she asks more than says.

"No. He won't come back."

And then the part I know is hardest for her to say.

"Babe, how do you know he was real?"

"How do I know *you're* real, Nuggins?" The moon now has full reign over the sky. "He just was."

BABE'S BLOG

I wake up to parental noises in the house. It surprises me at first until I remember they planned this day off together, the first one since we moved to Sugar Dunes, Florida.

We've still done practically nothing to make our house look like a home and I know they have a lot of errands to run.

I'm hoping they'll leave soon because I don't feel like talking this morning. Maybe if I'm quiet, they'll think I'm still asleep.

I open my laptop to check email, and then slip back into bed where I stare at the striped shadows on the wall.

It's starting to get hot and if they don't leave soon I'll be forced to turn on the AC, which will alert them to the fact I'm awake. But for now I just let my mind roam. Back to Zat and the last time we were together.

He was so quiet that day. And so sad. He behaved strangely from the very beginning. Did he know he was dying? Because I feel certain now that's what must have happened.

I think about the pine forest, and the thunderstorm. I remember how Earl came to us and took shelter under our umbrella. The picture he took—I wish I had it. But all I have is the picture Mai drew.

I get out of bed and tiptoe to the dresser where I keep Mai's picture. I bring it back into bed with me.

Why was Zat so rude to Earl? Was it because Earl intruded on a moment in time he already knew would be our last?

A surprising thought comes to me. A feeling. I had it once before when I lost my keys. I looked for them for two weeks and finally gave up. Mom was going out the next day to have duplicate house and car keys made for me. Then that feeling. This same feeling I'm having now. I got up in the middle of dinner without a word and walked into the next room, straight to the reclining chair I hardly ever sat on. Unofficially, it was Dad's, which was why I hadn't looked there before. I lifted the cushion of the chair and there were my keys, exactly where I knew they would be.

But I hadn't lost anything now.

Except Zat.

I *had* lost Zat.

And just like that it comes to me. Did Zat's confusing silence that night blind me to the expression in his eyes? When he looked at Earl, with what I thought was impatience, wasn't it awe? Wasn't it admiration?

Wasn't it . . . recognition?

Then, just as my subconscious led me to the keys under the cushion of the chair, it lifts my gaze to the picture above my bed. Of the small café with the green and yellow striped umbrellas, perched above the sand dunes and visible from the beach. What had Zat said to me? His last words . . .

"You'll never fail if you never try. But you'll never be happy either."

Someone else had said those words to me.

Earl had once said those words to me.

I scramble from bed and throw on a halter top and shorts. I slide into my flip flops and tie my uncombed hair into a bun on the back of my neck. I practically fly into the kitchen where my parents are sitting at the table, sipping coffee and buttering toast. Mom's still in her bathrobe. Her hair is mussed and her eyes are sleepy.

"Dad!" They both turn, surprised to see me barge in like this. "Where did you get the picture on my wall?"

He doesn't speak for a few seconds, his mind trying to make sense of my sudden crazy appearance and my interest in a photo he's probably long forgotten about. Then he realizes what picture.

"Oh, that one . . . I got it from Earl."

"He took that picture?"

"Yes. Photography's—"

"I know, a hobby of his. Do you know where he took it?"

"Sure. Lily's. Lily's Café over in Sand Harbor. I've been meaning to take you and your mother there one of these days. Earl says it's a real nice place for lunch and—"

"Dad," I interrupt him. "Could I have the keys to the truck?"

"Baby," Mom finally finds her voice. She's wondering what's come over me. "You know your father and I have been planning this day for a long time. We have a lot of things to do. We need the truck."

"Please! I'll be back in an hour. An hour and a half max." I know Sand Harbor's a thirty minute drive from us.

My dad looks at his watch. "You be back here by 11:30, no later." He's giving me two hours. He tosses the keys.

"Thanks, Dad." I throw my arms around his neck and kiss his rough, unshaven cheek.

"Promise?"

"I promise!"

Mom rolls her eyes, but I grab my purse and run out the door before they change their minds.

Earl is wise and charming In that *aw-shucks* country

kind of a way. I always thought of him as a nice guy, a guy you could count on if you needed to get a repairman out to your house.

Now I suspect Earl is something else. The camera which may not be a camera, after all. The photo above my bed that's appeared multiple times in my dreams. Is it a message? Is there something special about the café? A jumping off point maybe? And Earl showing up in my dream. Was it random or was he there to show Zat the way?

With all the pieces of the puzzle falling into place, I can't help but wonder if Earl is really Pioneer One.

I've never been to Sand Harbor before. It's smaller, more picturesque and touristy than Sugar Dunes. But as I'm driving through the town my energy and excitement evaporate.

When I find Lily's Café, I'm ready to turn around and go home. It's a real place. Real cars in the parking lot that faces the street. Real people coming and going. This couldn't be the place of my dreams, the place where I first saw Zat and felt the electricity of his presence. It's so ordinary—quaint, but ordinary. And Zat was anything but ordinary.

I don't even pull into the parking lot. I swing the truck around in a U-Turn and point myself back in the direction of home.

Despondent.

What was I thinking?

But then I remember what Zat said, "If you never try you'll never fail . . ." I keep driving until I see an area where I can pull off the road. I lock the truck and walk down to the beach.

It's a day like every other, but also like no other. Aquamarine waves spin lacy, white caps. The sky is a field of blue, the beach, a carpet of pearls.

I slip off my sandals and hold them in one hand. The talcum-like sand beneath my feet hasn't achieved the level of scorching it will reach later in the day. Already the early birds are here, unfolding beach chairs, laying down blankets, preparing surfside nests where the wave song will lull them into oblivion by the day's end.

The end of land. The beginning of sea. Which one will it be for me?

I could race down the beach to the place where I'm going but time can't change what will be, so I'll take my time. I'll walk slowly. I'll hold on to what might be the last moments when Zat is more than an impossible dream.

A young man and his wife stand knee deep in the water. Her belly is round like a ball, filled with their unborn child. He takes her hand and turns until they're facing each other. They smile at each other with promise and love.

I've intruded into their magic, which is so strong I can feel it even at this distance. It throws off sparks that rain down on me and make my eyes shine and burn with tears.

I'm almost there.

I know how far I've walked, so I know just when to look up toward the dunes. I see the umbrellas—colorfully striped, like zany mushrooms in a snow-covered pasture. This is where Earl must have stood when he framed his picture. I'll enter from here, from the place I remember.

Even the space between the two dunes is steep, steeper than I could tell from the picture.

I start to climb and the sand slips away beneath my feet. It's like scaling ice. Like walking up a downward escalator. With nothing to hang onto, I lose my footing and fall to my hands and knees.

A trickle of sand from above turns into a stream and I look up to locate its source.

And this time I'm not asleep.

His hair's thick and wavy, a light creamy brown. His eyes are that same shade of green as the sea oats. He smiles as though he's been expecting me and I shiver with recognition. I know this guy but I don't know him. Suddenly, I'm shy. Speechless. Awestruck.

He leans down to offer me his hand. "Let me help you," he says in a voice that's real and clear and strong.

He looks like Zat, but not exactly like the Zat of my dreams. He's slightly thinner, slightly paler, his eyes not quite as green, his hair not quite as flowing and thick. He's . . . real. Was it only a dream, after all?

"You're free now, Babe," he says when I don't take his hand.

He slides down the face of the dune until he's sitting beside me, nestled between the sea oats. "Your dreams are your own again."

"So it *is* you."

He doesn't answer, but instead looks beyond the beach toward the turquoise water of the Gulf.

"Everyone here is so happy," he says. "Everything is so much more beautiful than I could have imagined." He turns to face me. "You . . . you're so beautiful. It's overwhelming. Almost painful."

"Everyone's not happy." I reach over and take his hand in mine. It's warm. Real. "Everyone has problems, but that's part of life, isn't it?"

"Is it?" He seems so vulnerable, exposed, away from the safety of my dreams. And maybe he is. This is an alien landscape for him and he's here on his own. No, not on his own. With me. Forever. I know that now.

"You need a guide," I say gently. "Even pioneers have guides."

"Lewis and Clark had Sacagawea," he smiles.

"I came here looking for you, Zat," I say. "I want to be with you."

He cradles the side of my face with one hand, and then pulls me toward him, pressing his lips against mine. His fingers entwined in my hair sends a shiver racing up and down my spine. I'm reeling from the sight of him. The scent of him. The touch of him.

Comments:

DreamMe: Life is but a dream.

About the Author

Kathryn Berla is the author of *La Casa 758* (Penguin Random House, Spain) and the YA romance, *12 Hours in Paradise*. Her novel, *Dream Me*, will be released by Amberjack Publishing in July 2017. *The House at 758*, an English translation of *La Casa 758*, will be released by Amberjack Publishing October 2017.

Kathryn loves to write about whatever happens to float through her mind and linger long enough to become an obsession. Her interests vary; hence, her genres range from sci-fi to horror to contemporary literary fiction.

When she's not obsessing over an untold story percolating in her brain, Kathryn can be found walking pretty much anywhere, doing Pilates, or catching up on episodes of *The Walking Dead*, *Girls*, *Westworld*, and . . . well, too many others to name here. She has been an avid movie buff since childhood, and she often sees the movie in her head before she writes the book.

As a State Department brat, Kathryn grew up in India, Syria, Europe, and Africa, and the love of seeing new places still runs deep. She gives into it whenever she can.

Kathryn loves dolphins, owls, elephants, warm beaches, and especially warm summer nights. A warm summer night where she could sit on a beach and see an owl, dolphin, or elephant would be her preferred method of passing time.

Kathryn graduated from the University of California in Berkeley with a degree in English, but she takes the most pride in having studied creative writing under Walter van Tilburg Clark at the University of Nevada. She likes to brag that she had the same translator in Spain as John Green.

She currently lives in the beautiful San Francisco Bay Area, which she would never leave because she can't think of another place with as much to offer, including the proximity of her entire family. She lives with her three sons and husband, who are her most constant muses, sounding boards, and general cheerleaders and critics. They normally don't complain too much about these enforced roles.

Acknowledgements

First and foremost, thank you to George Berla, my husband and real life Dream Boy.

Thank you to Amberjack Publishing for turning this dream into a reality. Dayna, Kayla, Cherrita, and Cami. You guys all rock and I couldn't have asked for a better team behind me.

Multiple thanks (too many to count) to Corey, Lucas, and Jeremy Berla for your love, support, feedback, glitch-fixing, and general superior-sons' abilities. And to Samantha Berla, a daughter at last.

And thank you to the real main character of my book, Florida's beautiful panhandle coastline and its lovely inhabitants who are lucky enough to be able to wriggle their toes in the sugar-white sand whenever the fancy strikes them.

And thank you for the beautiful blue orb that more than 7 billion of us call home. May you live long and always be a haven for dreams past, present, and future.